Trickle Down Theory

A MMMM WHY CHOOSE ROMANCE

from the world of

Will Forrest

A NOTE FOR READERS

zečić - "bunny" (Croatian)

For readers' mental and emotional well-being, the following list highlights any sensitive or potentially triggering subjects depicted or referred to in this book.

If you do not experience distress while reading sensitive subjects, I invite you to skip this page.

Either way, happy reading and stay safe!

This book is for mature audiences. It depicts explicit sexual activity between consenting adult partners, including a consensual 'Primal Play' chase-and-capture scene.

Characters experience or make reference to the following:

- eating disorder (bulimia)

- anxiety disorder

- panic attacks

- internalized homophobia

- past experience of bullying

- hostile childhood environment

- toxic self-image

Chapter 28 contains the following:

- homophobic language

- stress-induced vomiting

Please Read Responsibly

TRICKLE DOWN THEORY

Just because you watch gay porn doesn't mean you're gay...

Sure, you can tell yourself that if you want to, but some of you would be better off admitting how much you like the idea of another guy wrecking you. Making you crave him. Making you beg him to fuck you. Loving every minute of it when he does. Then wanting even more.

I wanted more. I've done enough work on myself by now to be comfortable admitting how greedy I am. How needy. How desperately I depend on other people's praise to feel like I'm worth anything. I'll never shake it, even now that I know it's a trauma response. I'll always be emotionally dependent on other people to make me feel alive.

The trick is finding people who love to give. Who like to be in control, for when I go off the rails. Who want nothing more than a needy little brat to tame, to keep.

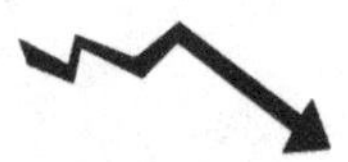

I didn't know any of this at the time. Back then, I was still pretending that I wasn't gay. That the fact that I'd had sex with women meant I had to be heterosexual. Never mind that I was usually either high or drunk or both at the time, that the women were usually the friends of women my friends were dating, dragged along to the club and so bored that leaving with me seemed like an improvement.

At least I had a nice condo to take them to, with an amazing view of the lake from the living room, across the roof of the Rogers Center so no one was ever going to build in front of me and block the sightline. Quartz counters in the kitchen I never used. Hardwood flooring and recessed lighting and in-unit washer/dryer, which I also never used because as if I was going to wash my own clothes when I could pay someone else to do it.

Outsource Everything: one of the most important rules in the game of Being Rich. I thought that living as if I was money was the easiest way to attract it. That I could afford to mortgage my future, because the payout was going to be so huge. That the economy worked the way I'd been taught in all those podcasts and blogs and the Wall Street Journal.

I was a change-maker in the making.

I was going to win the world.

THE WALLET

REAGAN

I'M GOING TO GET fired one of these days...

Not what I like to be thinking right before I nut, but there's only so much porn you can watch on company time before the guilt sets in. Instead of making me stop, it makes me jerk myself faster, trying to beat the guy on the screen, get off before he does.

I've lost count of how many dicks the bottom has had rammed down his pretty throat. That's the point, though. That's why I barely have to click in the search bar these days for the site to start serving me cock-sucking videos.

As the top pushes the twink off him and starts to jerk himself I blow, my come soaking through the handful of tissues as the actor's come spurts onto that twink's messy face. I turn up the audio and leave it playing, the sloppy moaning echoing around the empty room as I go wash my hands and dick and grab another can of energy drink. All I do in this condo is work and sleep and eat takeaway, so I've kept the furnishing minimal. It's easier for the cleaner too, so I don't have to tip her as much. Outsource everything, because my time is too valuable to waste on keeping house when I could be using it to make more money.

I set the empty drink can on top of the pyramid forming beside my chair, then log into my crypto account. Or at least I try. Fuck these long password strings, though how cut and paste could drop a digit...

Shit.

I try again. Then again. One more time, and then I stop. Because there's a limit. Too many attempts and they lock your wallet for good. All that money, gone...

My hands are shaking as I open my phone to message Mitch. If he changed the password and didn't tell me, I'm going to lose it. Except I can't message him because it bounces. Someone I text ten, twenty times a day suddenly doesn't exist. I hop to another app, then another, but it's like he was never there. Like he doesn't want to be found. But I'm not panicking yet.

It takes me opening my email and sending a mail to every address he's ever had, and getting bounced every time, for me to start panicking.

u seen mitch? I DM to our friend Lin.

n

u sure?

y

can't find him in my contacts and his mails bounced wtf?

...

...

...

I wait, watching those grey dots repopulate again and again. What kind of epic reply is Lin writing? What does he know that I don't?

haven't seen him, he replies.

Bullshit. I put my phone down and start pacing again. There's an easy explanation. I'm in the wrong email program, an account I never use. Or I spelt 'Mitch' wrong. My best friend and investment partner has not disappeared off the face of the earth, taking all of our money with him.

He wouldn't. I might, but Mitch wouldn't. Mitch isn't that smart. Mitch doesn't have that cut-throat instinct.

Mitch...Mitch is a fucking liar and I'm a dumbass.

I'm sweating now. Badly, the mouse slipping against my damp palm as I scroll back through our correspondence looking for any clue that he was about to go dark, but there's nothing. Just shitposting and AI nudes, stock forecasts, IPOs, and pictures of luxury cars. No sign that he was about to fuck me in the ass, dry. Fucker didn't even buy me dinner first.

I laugh, because otherwise I'm going to puke. I'm probably going to do that anyway, the energy drink burning in my stomach, my heart threatening to break through my ribs. If I don't get that money back, I can kiss my life goodbye.

My bank laughed at me. So did the guy at Canada Revenue, though he hid it better. The cops won't return my calls, and no one's heard from Mitch. Or they're lying to me. Maybe he paid them off. It doesn't matter, the end result is the same. I've lost eight hundred and sixty two thousand dollars. About fifteen grand of which was never mine.

I don't remember the last time I slept. Or ate. All I do is scroll for answers. Every answer is the same: I'm screwed. Blockchain is the best form of security, until it's the fucking worst. My eyes burning from staring at the screen, I push back from my desk, letting my arms dangle as my chair slowly rotates across the bare laminate. The day is long over, the sunset shooting long rays of ruby light between the condos to the west, and I'm about to wheel myself to the bathroom for a sleeping pill when my phone buzzes. I snatch it up, praying without faith for it to be Mitch. I'd even talk to my parents. Anyone but Paladin Investment's CEO Ajay. My boss.

You know I don't like spyware he's written, because he's been watching me do no work at all for days.

sorry I know I haven't done shit this week got some personal stuff going down

that's fine but don't leave me hanging

I know I'm sorry it's been brutal

can you spare a couple hours for an in office

I should say no. I'm already fucked, so I should just say no. Quit right now, effective immediately. Be a fucking man and take action to protect myself.

no worries I text back. *tomorrow ok?*

We pick a time. Then I put my phone on airplane mode, get up from my chair with a groan because when the fuck did I last stand up, go to the bathroom and dry-swallow an Ambien. Otherwise I will lie awake all night wondering whether Ajay is going to mention the fourteen thousand seven hundred and twelve dollars in arbitrary expenses piggybacking on the budget from that conference we all went to in Germany.

Waking up the next day sucks, as if I'm an action figure who's had all his limbs pulled off and has to put himself back together. Cradling my last can of energy drink like *my precioussss* I huddle in the back of the Uber trying not to hurl.

Maybe this meeting won't be a big deal. Maybe Ajay just wants to check in. A wellness check, after all that shit HR has been talking about work-life balance and the burnout epidemic in the financial sector. I keep telling myself this all the way to the office, but somehow when I toss the empty drink can in the trash in the lobby, every bit of my confidence goes with it.

Ajay knows. He knows I stole that money. He knows I lost it too, though I'm not sure how that's possible. Sweating, shaking, I force myself to move one foot and then the other until I'm on the elevator. I stand close to the door, and too fucking bad if I'm in the way. I can't give myself the slightest chance to avoid getting off the elevator.

Someone else gets off at the eighteenth floor and I let their movement lead me. As I approach the front desk the receptionist looks up long enough to clock my lanyard, then goes back to ignoring me. A few people nod as I pass their desks, but most of the open office floor is empty. Ajay's office is in the far corner. The door is open a bit, and when I knock he calls me in.

I never see this man sweat. I've never heard him raise his voice higher than a teacher's calm attention-getting *I'm going to need you all to settle down*. He's the best boss I've ever had and probably ever will, I realize as I ease the door closed behind me.

"What's up?" I ask.

"You tell me," Ajay says, his thick brows pinching as he looks me up and down. "What happened to you, Reagan? You look terrible."

"I know. I've had some super bad news."

"No one died, did they?" he asks gently, as if he might actually care.

"No. I, um, lost some money. A lot of money. I got conned."

"That's not a good look for an asset manager," he says, shaking his head.

"No shit. Sorry. I don't mean to be rude, but he wiped me out. It's pretty much all I can think about."

"I get it," Ajay says, folding his hands on the desk. "If you need to take some personal time while you deal with it, then go ahead. But I don't like people wasting company time."

"Right. Sure. I'll talk to HR."

"Oh, and one more thing," he says casually as I feel behind me for the door handle. "I've been asking around but no one has an answer for me. About this overage on the Frankfurt budget."

I wait too long to answer, and as his face hardens I know I'm fucked. He takes a deep breath, closing his eyes as he exhales and lets his head fall back against the pillowy leather of his executive chair.

"I'm fired, aren't I?" I ask when I find my voice.

"Oh yeah," he says, his eyes still closed. "Now I'm just trying to figure out if it's worth calling the cops. I'd sue you but you don't have any money, so what's the point? Don't. Fucking. Apologize," he says, putting his hand up to halt me as I take a breath. "Seriously, I don't want to hear another word out of you ever again. You can't fix this, Reagan. So just go. If you see me out in public, no you fucking didn't."

There's a million things I want to say. None of them will make him change his mind, so I do what I'm told for a change and I shut my mouth and leave his office. I've got about five minutes before he gets security to walk me out, so I dip to my cubicle, where I shovel everything that isn't nailed down into the wastepaper basket, then leave by the fire stairs.

The fire is me.

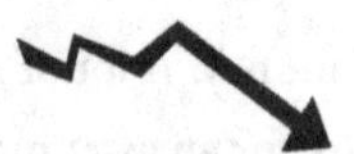

I walk and I walk, until the office building has shrunk to a single digit among the handfuls of silvery fingers rising along University Ave and my arms ache from carrying the wastepaper bin. I don't even remember what's in it. Ignoring the homeless guy lying on a sheet of cardboard under the bushes, I set down the bin on the bench at the next bus stop to sort through the contents.

A stapler, a stack of sticky notes, a handful of pens and markers; a mousepad and the cordless mouse, but not the USB that connects it to the computer; my U of T Economics hoodie with the frayed cuffs and the bleach stain on the back; a can of sugar-free Red Bull. My severance package. No, my severance is not getting the cops called on my dumb ass.

For a second I'm sure I'm going to be sick, but I'm standing in the middle of downtown Toronto. There's no fucking way I'm going to let these randos see me fall apart. I stuff the bin of useless crap into the trash can beside the bench.

"Aw man," the homeless dude says, shoving himself upright. "I would have taken that off your hands."

"It's all yours," I say, gesturing to the trash can.

"Gee, thanks," he says dryly. "Asshole," he adds under his breath as he starts to get up.

"You know what, here," I say, unstrapping my three-month old Breitling Superocean Heritage B20 Automatic 42 from my wrist. "You can have this too."

"Dude," he breathes, looking from me to the gleaming watch in my hand and back. He's not much older than me, his face blistered by sunburn, his hair an unwashed brown mop. Cautiously he puts out his hand to take the watch, his eyes widening at the weight of it. "Are you dying or something?"

"I fucking hope so."

I've got a couple hundred in cash on me, so I go into the next bar I pass and start drinking. Three shots of terrible tequila and two decent craft brews later, I'm ready to call my dealer, but if I start in on the coke I'll end up draining my bank account. So I keep drinking, as the bar fills up around me with happy people who haven't torched their career or been ripped off by someone they trusted. Or maybe they have and I'm just the loser who can't get over his problems.

I leave when the band starts playing. I hate live music. It's too loud and the sound is always trash and people who go to concerts are boring. It's nighttime now, and every third place is a fucking concert venue, crowds of fashion-phobic people standing around blocking the sidewalk, breathing their vapes in my face. All the other shops are dark, like the sky is dark like asphalt is dark like my future.

When I finally reach a club that's playing music that doesn't completely suck, I go inside, shove some money at the emo chick at the ticket table, then ask her to point me towards the bar.

DUMPED

CARTER

It should have been a boring break up. It should have happened a month ago. I should have known when Trey wanted to go to Amanuensis that this was our last date.

I don't know what it is about Amanuensis but I know more people who have been dumped there than at any other restaurant in town. Because ordering a hundred and fifty bucks' worth of food and drink is such a good opener when you're planning to ruin someone's day.

"What the hell, Trey?" I say, putting down my knife and fork. I haven't splurged on a steak in ages, and now there's every chance I won't get to eat another bite. "Is this really how you want this to end?"

"Be honest with yourself, Carter. You know we're going nowhere," he replies with a pout, toying with his stemless wine glass as he glances around the dimly lit restaurant.

"So why did you make me come—you know what, you're right. This was never going to last."

"We're just not connecting," he says with a simpering grin. "I mean, obviously the sex has been great, but it's just not enough for me."

"Maybe if you put in a bit of effort—ugh, I don't care. I'm not going to fight to save something neither of us want." The waitress is about to pass so I drain my beer and signal to her to bring me another. Break up or no break up, I'm eating this steak.

"Well good," Trey says as I pick up my cutlery. "I thought this would be a lot harder."

"We gave it a shot, and it didn't work out."

"So I guess it's no big deal that I slept with Gregor last night," he says into his glass.

I put down my cutlery again with a clatter. "I'm sorry, you did what?"

"It doesn't matter what I did," he says, mumbling over the rim of the glass. "We just broke up."

"Yeah, but we hadn't then."

"What difference does it make?"

"You cheated on me!"

"But we were going to break up," he says through his teeth, glancing at the diners at the tables around us.

"Which means you're a chickenshit too. You slept with Gregor so I'd be pissed off and dump you, and you wouldn't have to act like a grown up."

"Hello? We decided to stop seeing each other *mutually*."

"And you sat there lying to my face while we did it."

Fuck the steak. Fuck Troy *with* the steak, the lying little shit. Before I say anything I'll regret, I get to my feet.

"That won't cover everything," he whines as I throw a fifty on the table.

"You can send me an invoice for the balance. Care of go fuck yourself."

Here comes the waitress with my beer. She hesitates, but I take it from her tray and drink half the pint in a few swallows. The petty little queen in me wants to throw the other half of the beer in Trey's face and ruin his makeup, but I settle for throwing a twenty on the waitress' tray. I drain the glass, set it on the table, then leave the restaurant. Carefully, because I shouldn't have drank two pints in five minutes on a mostly empty stomach.

It's a pretty night, without the humidity we had last week, and when I reach Trinity Bellwoods Park I turn onto Crawford Street to cut along the side. Though a few people are strolling the paths, most of them with dogs, I like to give the unhoused population who are using the park plenty of space, so I usually stick to the perimeter after dark.

As I'm passing the recreation center, a man lurches out of the shadows under the trees. Not one of the unhoused people I've spoken to but a white guy in his mid-twenties with frosted hair, wearing a pink polo with a popped collar and blue trousers that bare his ankles and show off his Prada trainers. He's so drunk I can smell him, and I take a step back as he grabs for my arm.

"Let me suck you off," he slurs.

"What?"

"I said—"

"I heard you, but—"

"Please," he gasps, snatching for my arm again.

"Dude, you're drunk."

"Duh. Come on, you know you want a piece." He licks his lips. Wide, pouting lips that shouldn't interest me at all. "Hundred bucks to pop this cherry."

Finally, a way to bring this to an end. "I don't have a hundred bucks," I say with a laugh.

He pulls a handful of money out of his pocket—fives, tens, a twenty or two—and as I stand there in shock he yanks down my collar and shoves the bills down the front of my shirt. "You do now."

I'm too stunned to argue and just drunk enough not to give a damn as he grabs my hand and drags me into the wedge of darkness between the community center sign and a wall of shrubbery. He smells spoiled, like fruit left to rot, like sweet skin and sour liquor as he backs me against a tree then drops to his knees in front of me.

Fumbling drunkenly, he manages to get my jeans open, but as he tries to get my dick out through the front of my briefs it's clear he has no idea what he's doing down there. I obviously have no idea what I'm doing either, because I should be stopping him. I shouldn't be easing my erection out of my underwear for a total stranger to suck as we hide in the bushes outside the rec center. But then he figures out how to get his mouth around my cock, and forgive me but I stop caring about anything else.

Maybe I was wrong. Maybe he does this a lot, because he takes me so deep I think he's swallowed me. Biting my lip so I don't start yelling, I put my hand on his head, his stiffly gelled hair crunching under my touch. He whimpers around me, leaning into it even more, grabbing my hip with his free hand.

I want to own his mouth, own him, and he whimpers again as my grip tightens in his sharp locks. I shouldn't want any of this, but I can't make myself stop. Not with the way he sucks me. Deep and hard, his cheeks hollowing, dirty little noises leaking out of his throat. I twitch my hips and his whole body stiffens, his throat opening even more. He wants the same thing I do, and with one hand locked in his hair I begin to pump into his drooling mouth.

His nails scrabble at the fabric of my jeans, his other hand dropping from my thigh to disappear into the darkness, his body rocking in rhythm with mine as I fuck his mouth, the head of my cock driving deep into his throat. It's the sluttiest thing I've ever done and maybe the stupidest too but I can't stop, won't stop, couldn't if I wanted to as I come, groaning through my teeth as pleasure rips through me. Yet the minute he tastes it he jerks back, taking most of my load in his face.

He shouts, some mashed up drunken obscenity, his body convulsing. Did I make him come too by creaming on him? I can't speak, can barely move as he lurches to his feet. And then he's gone, his footsteps slapping against the pavement until they're lost in the sounds of the night.

What the fuck just happened?

Dazed, diminished, I put my limp, stinging cock away and creep out from behind the sign. The street is empty of pedestrians, and I'm about to flee the scene when I notice a five dollar bill lying on the sidewalk. There's another, and a handful of change, and a few feet away a skinny leather wallet.

"Holy shit. He dropped loot."

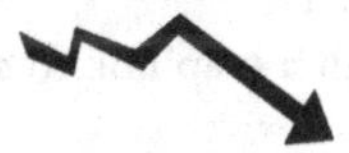

The next morning I'm at the public health clinic as soon as it opens. Me and a mixed bag of other horn-dogs who are dumb enough to have had risky sex last night but are smart enough not to deny it. Everyone in the waiting room keeps their eyes on their phones in case they turn out to know each other.

As I wait I can't keep from replaying the whole thing in my mind. The smell of him, the fact that *he* paid *me*. The scrape of the bark against my back and the scratch of his product-laden hair beneath my hand. I wonder if he did get off just from sucking me. I should stop thinking about it, because if he lied, if that wasn't the first blow job he'd ever given, if he drooled his toxic drool all over my knock-on-wood never-had-an-STI junk...I'll have no one to blame but myself.

I feel nauseous until they text me the results a few hours later: clear across the board. Maybe he really was a virgin. Or maybe I just got lucky, a terrible joke once I think about it. And that guy is still a weirdo. Probably some closeted 'elite male' with a secret Grindr account. Who even cares, all I have to do is give him back his wallet and then I never have to see him again.

Sitting on my bed, half wishing I had tossed the wallet in the nearest mailbox and made it Canada Post's problem, I text the number on the hyper expensive square matte black business card: *did you or someone you know lose a wallet at the trinity bellwoods rec center last night?*

I've barely switched apps when the reply comes: *y*

"Ugh, he's one of those." *Where do you want to meet?*

? u?

"Oh my god…" I flop back on my bed. I do not have the energy for this middle school shit. My phone buzzes with another message

this ok? He follows with a map link to a little park down by the esplanade.

sure what's a good time?

wyd?

"Checking the transit tracker app, I guess." I've known this guy for all of fifteen minutes and he's already the most annoying person alive. With the streetcar under construction it's faster for me to head up to Bloor and take the airport train down to Union Station, but that's public transit in Toronto: a glorified city bus trying to serve two point five million people.

We agree to meet in half an hour. Kid's lucky he didn't give me herpes or I'd be on my way not to give him back his wallet but to punch him in the face. Except I would never. Because I don't go low. And I'm not wearing an assault charge for this idiot. I'll just give him his wallet and a few words of warning from an elder gay, then never see his gelled hair, flood pant, popped collar-wearing ass again.

BOOT-HEELS OF THE REVOLUTION

REAGAN

I WASN'T PREPARED FOR how hot he is. This guy whose dick I paid to suck, on my knees in the dark. I shouldn't be thinking about that, but he's making me want to do it again, with those tattooed forearms, those melting brown eyes, the spray of grey hair salting the closely cut sides of his head.

All I've done since yesterday is think about being gay. About all the reasons I ever pretended that I wasn't: my parents, my friends, my ideals, my prejudices. But if God existed, He was already putting me through hell, so how could it get any worse?

Don't laugh.

Okay, you can laugh a little bit because I feel myself get hard just looking at him, this guy I can never have, because I fucked up his first impression of me. Hoping he can't see my erection, I stay sitting on the bench as he approaches then sits down beside me.

"Thanks for not throwing it out," I say as he hands me my wallet.

"No problem."

I expect him to get up and leave, but he stays seated, looking me over like Ajay did. Then he sighs, slinging his arm over the back of the bench to look at me directly. "I know we're strangers, but can I give you some advice?"

"Go ahead."

"It's half on me for not stopping you, but you can't be going around sucking guys off without some protection. You do not want to catch what's out there."

"I know. I was out of my head."

"That was obvious, but you can't let that be an excuse. If you're that fucked up, you shouldn't be having sex of any kind. Drunk consent isn't real consent."

"I just read that somewhere. Actually that's pretty much all I've been doing. Reading, podcasts, blogs, whatever. Trying to educate myself, right?"

"About what?"

"Think what you want, but I'd never done any gay shit before."

"So you weren't kidding about that cherry."

The way his lip curls as he says it makes my butt clench. This would be so much easier if he wasn't hot. I would have taken my wallet, taken my medicine for hooking up with a troll, and gone on with my life. Instead I'm blushing like a little bitch, wishing he would either leave or demand that I suck him again.

"I didn't mean to tease you," he says softly. "Virginity's no big deal, no matter what anyone tells you."

"What? Right. Sure. Thanks." Fuck, he's going to think I'm an idiot. He'd be right, but as my face heats he frowns.

"You don't have to tell me, but are you okay?" he asks.

"I'm fine. Some stuff happened kind of all at once but I'm fine."

"I'm happy to listen if you want to talk about it."

"No, I'm fine. I don't want to put my shit on you."

"I'm a big boy, I can take it."

I'm fine. I'm not fucked. I haven't fucked up my whole life, I haven't nearly been charged with fraud, lost my job and all my money, and learned my best friend was a grifting piece of shit. "I made some enemies, I guess. Someone I thought was my friend locked my crypto wallet, and I don't know how to get it back. Plus I kind of loaned myself some money from my boss to buy the coins, so he fired me and threatened to sue me and/or turn me into the cops, and now I'm pretty much broke and totally screwed. And you're fucking laughing at me. Great, I'm so glad I shared this with you."

Seriously laughing, bent over double, clutching his stomach. "Sorry, but dude..." He stops to wipe his eyes. "You're a case study of the failure of crypto currency."

"What are you talking about, failure? I made thousands. Tens of thousands."

"And lost it all in a couple keystrokes. I bet your bank told you to go fuck yourself."

"I knew the risks."

"Are you sure?"

"All investments have an element of risk."

He rolls his eyes. "Dude, bitcoin is not an investment. It's gambling. It's astrology for tech bros."

"It's a financial instrument."

"It's a Ponzi scheme."

"What even is that?"

"Dude..." Still chuckling, he grabs his forehead like it hurts. The prick is laughing at my pain.

"Look, it's not even your business," I say, hating the way my voice rises when I'm angry.

"You're right," he says, trying to straighten his face. "I shouldn't laugh, it sounds like you're in a bad place. I just don't meet a lot of people like you."

"Why, are all your friends woke?"

He snorts a laugh. "The fact that you asked that proves that you aren't."

"Of course I'm not. Bunch of losers whining about nothing."

"And this is why I don't hang out with people like you. You don't have a fucking clue."

"Just admit you're broke."

"I know I'm broke. But I'm also not delusional."

Is he trying to piss me off? If only he wasn't hot, because then I could tell him to go fuck himself. Instead that dark stare is making me want to throw myself at him, fall at his feet right here in the park in front of the dog walkers and the executives on their phones.

"Exactly how am I delusional?" I ask, trying to keep my voice level. "All I did was put some money in an investment vehicle known for paying high returns. That's how the economy works."

"No, it doesn't."

"What are you, an economist?"

"I don't need to be to know that crypto's a pyramid scheme. It depends on an endless supply of suckers."

"I'm not a sucker!" I am however yelling in the park. I take a deep breath and exhale slowly, thinking about those videos HR made us watch about diversity and thinking before you speak. "Okay, so crypto isn't a sure bet but what is? We're all taking chances just by being alive. And at least I'm out here doing something, trying to get ahead instead of settling for mediocrity."

"Oh god, here we go," he groans, letting his head fall back.

"You're damn right, here we go, with you coming along all high and mighty, just because you never had the balls to roll the fucking dice. You gotta be in it to win it."

He chuckles, grabbing his forehead again. "Who still says that? Are you going to make me bust out my TedX talk about the economic delusion?"

"The what?"

"The belief you weirdos have that economic growth is a good in and of itself and that it alone is the driver of social progress."

"What else makes change happen?"

"Revolution. Power to the people, man." Grinning, he pumps his arm, the stretch of his sleeve around his bicep making me shiver. But I don't care how hot he is. He's the one with the delusion.

"I get what's going on here. You're a socialist."

He only smiles wider. "So what if I am? Can you blame me? Capitalism only values me to the extent I play its game. But deep down, the powers that be would be happier if gay men didn't exist. What good are we if we're not breeding more wage slaves?"

"Is that what you really think?"

"Based on the evidence. You can believe what you want, tech bro, but if you'd paid any attention in history class you'd know the only way we change the world for the better is from the bottom up. Time after time, every concession made by capital to the rights of the common people, people have had to take by force. Grab capital by the throat and squeeze."

As he crushes his hand into a fist I realize I'm staring. Staring at his hand, the flexing of his long fingers, the cords standing out in his wrists, the tiny star tattooed on the base of his middle finger. I want that hand on me, wrapping around my cock, my throat. Holding me still while the rest of him...

"Sorry, what did you say?"

"I said, is my revolutionary zeal turning you on?"

"A little." A lie, as his hungry smile makes my balls clench.

"You like the thought of being trampled under the boot-heels of the revolution?" he continues in a brain-erasing purr. "Shoved against the wall, helpless to stop the tidal forces of history from taking what they want from you?"

"Holy fuck," I breathe, wiping my sweating palms on my jeans. "Can we go somewhere and...I don't live far from here."

He gazes at me, weighing his options. I want to beg, throw my pride aside and beg for it. I shouldn't be this needy, shouldn't want to give in so soon. Shouldn't be this open with someone I just met, someone I'm so different from that we'll never have more than this moment, but I've never wanted anything—anyone—so badly in my life. A life that I've spent wanting things, chasing wealth because it's the next best thing to power. And I want him more. Want him standing over me, his dick down my throat, his come on my face.

"You don't ever have to see me again," I say as he takes a deep breath.

He lets it go with a sigh, shaking his head. "I can't believe I'm doing this."

THE CONDO

CARTER

REALLY, I CAN'T BELIEVE it. I don't do this sort of shit. Which is why I'm going to do it, because I never would.

Can't I make wrong choices now and then? I know it's a terrible idea, getting anywhere near this twitchy little tech bro. But his mouth is gorgeous, his lips trembling with anticipation, his eyes pleading.

And I'm no monk. It's nice to be wanted. Nice: it's a fucking ego boost, right when I need it. He's several inches and at least thirty pounds lighter than me so I'm not in any danger from him as he leads me to one of those shiny new condo developments by the Rogers Centre. A woman with a chihuahua on a retractable leash is already on the elevator, and when she sees the guy she scoops up the dog. She glares at us the whole ride, getting off one floor below.

"A friend of yours?" I joke as we walk down the hall.

"Her dog bit me a few months ago. She's still pissed I told the condo board."

"Why did it bite you?"

"I don't know. Maybe because it's an untrained rat with a brain the size of a walnut."

"You hate dogs too? No wonder you don't have any friends."

"Look, if you're just going to insult me–"

"Sorry. Again." What the fuck is my problem? Just because we're political opposites doesn't mean he doesn't have human emotions. As much as the conservative agenda seems to hinge on not having any.

Then we get to his unit and my heart nearly breaks, because the guy has nothing. A big empty room with a million dollar view and not a single piece of furniture. No bookshelves, no stereo, no art on the walls. A room and a view.

"So you really did lose everything," I murmur, turning around once more, my voice ringing off the hard surfaces.

"You think I was making it up?"

"No, just...what some people think of as losing everything is really only being mildly inconvenienced. You, on the other hand..."

"I'm fucked, right?"

"It doesn't look great."

"Doesn't matter. I'll be out of this place soon."

"Then what?"

"I don't know. Look, can we just fuck instead of talking about how badly I screwed up?" He's already untying the drawstring on his executive track pants.

"Slow down, bro. There's a couple of things to sort out."

"It's cool if we just do what we did the first time."

"I meant things like what's your name?"

"It's Reagan. I'm twenty six, I'm allergic to penicillin, and I hate my parents. What else do you need to know?"

"Why you were hiding in the bushes outside the rec center looking for guys to blow."

"Because I was shit-faced."

"Yeah, but why did you want to do it in the first place?"

"Because I have nothing left to lose. So why not come out? Be fucking honest about myself for once and say I like dick." He's vibrating, his voice tight with emotion as he spits out the words.

"You're coming out for the first time, aren't you. Like right now."

"No. Yes, maybe, I don't know. Can't you just fuck me?"

"No."

"What?" he blurts, his eyes flying open. "Why not?"

"Because you're a mess. And you know you can just *be* gay, right? You don't have to prove anything to me to be able to claim the label."

"This isn't about you."

"And that's another reason I don't want to fuck you. Other than the fact that I barely know you."

"That didn't matter to you last night."

"Because I was drunk too. I should have said no."

"Are you seeing anyone?"

"Why, are you asking me out?"

He doesn't quite answer, shrugging as he spreads his hands. Brave enough to want it but not brave enough to say it. But do I want it? Do I want to put my time into someone who's going to fight me on every issue that matters to me? Or is that my own prejudice speaking, my residual shame from high school mingling with my political rage from undergrad making me judge this guy based on one conversation and one reckless fuck?

"I'll think about it, okay?" I say. "I'm not saying there isn't some kind of vibe here, but I don't know if I can deal with all the rest."

"What do you mean, the rest?" he says, dodging in front of me as I start for the door. "What's wrong with me?"

"Nothing. But you might not like me as much, once you get to know me. Not for who I am but for what I believe."

"I'd get over it."

"Would you?"

"I'd try."

"I don't want a partner who only tolerates me. He has to accept me. There's ethical points that I won't budge on. Questions I always ask someone I'm seeing. You might have to confront some hard truths about yourself."

"You think I'm not doing that already?" Reagan replies, gesturing around us. "What you see is all I have left, and I won't even have this soon. Please, give me something to look forward to. Something to make it worth getting up tomorrow."

He's staring at me with that same humming intensity as before, like he's going to shatter if I say the wrong thing. If I turn him down, am I going to read a headline tomorrow about him jumping in front of a train?

"Fine. We'll give it a shot. Text me and we'll work something out."

We swap numbers, so at last he knows my name. His tense posture suggests he's not a hugger, so I leave it at that. Leave him to his nothingness, alone in the empty apartment.

I'm barely on the streetcar when his first text message arrives: *thanks again it was great to connect with you and I'm looking forward to the next time.*

Like he met me at a conference and is trying to solidify his network. I reply with a thumbs up, which is a mistake. I should have left it on read, because by the time I get home he's sent twenty more texts. Has Reagan never made a friend before?

The message thread is half a resume, half a confession: every school he attended, every extra-curricular thing he was in, his gay awakening (of last night, for fuck's sake), and every way he tried to deny it until now. With each notification I wonder why I'm bothering. I stopped replying ten messages back but he keeps writing, until I know all about the only time he went to summer camp but had to leave on the third day because he freaked out so badly.

My phone buzzes again as I'm climbing my front steps: *but maybe im bi or pan because idk some ppl are just hot yk how do you find that stuff out is there like a quiz i can do?*

"I can't take any more of this," I mutter, thumbing my reply. I'll either shame him into action, or piss him off enough he'll leave me alone:

MY BROTHER IN CHRIST I AM NOT YOUR THERAPIST

u think I need to go too?

probably. it helped me.

ok thx

I stand there for nearly a minute staring at my phone, waiting for his next message, my keys in my other hand, my brain on fire, before I realize he's not going to reply. If only he wasn't such a snack, even with the frosted hair.

If only I didn't believe in giving people second chances.

THERAPY

REAGAN

Therapy is fucking expensive. But I look for a therapist anyway, doing eight free video consults before I land on someone who doesn't drown me in feminist rhetoric or obsess over my internalized homophobia. What I want is actionable steps towards becoming emotionally intelligent, not sob sessions about my daddy being mean to me.

Dr. Whitman's office looks like a therapist's office from the movies, with bookshelves and a bay window and one of those buttoned leather couches you can lie on, though I'm good to sit. Whitman himself is perfectly cast, with a bald head but a kind smile and rectangular frameless glasses that leave a pink dent on each side of his long nose when he takes them off to polish them partway through me telling him about the time I blacked out at the provincial debate finals.

"Before we go any further," he says, hooking his glasses on the front of his argyle vest. "I wanted to talk a little bit about what therapy can and cannot do for people."

"I'm obviously not asking you for business advice," I say, sticking my hands under my thighs so I'll stop picking my nails.

"Of course not. I'm afraid quite a lot of what you told about your work went right over my head. So may I ask you instead why you decided to try therapy?"

Don't tell him it's because you want to get railed. "A friend recommended it."

"Was that all it took to persuade you?"

"I respect him a lot, respect his opinion and stuff. If he thinks it will help me then it's probably worth it."

"And what do you hope to get out of our sessions?"

To learn how to be a normal person. To figure out what's wrong with me. To find the heart of all my mistakes and fucking detonate it.

"It's okay if you don't have an answer right now," he says as I sit there shaking like an idiot, or more like the idiot I obviously am. "Sounds like you have a lot to unpack."

"No shit," I blurt. "Sorry. This is a lot harder than I thought it would be."

"Trust me, I know," Whitman says with a chuckle, crossing his legs. "I fought therapy for years. Refused to admit how badly I needed an outlet for my own difficult thoughts. I wouldn't trust a therapist who wasn't willing to humble themselves, to be honest."

"I always thought there was something wrong with people who went to therapy."

"In a sense, there is. That's why we're here, to heal."

"Right. That makes sense. Wow, I'm not..." I cover my mouth as the truth hits like a kick in the guts, my chest burning as the bile rises. Of course there's something wrong with me, like there always has been.

"You know, I'm kind of starting to think I'm not as smart as I think I am," I gulp. "Fuck, that sounds so stupid. What the fuck am I doing?" Not just in the moment but in every moment of my wasted fucking life.

Eighty five thousand dollars in tuition and that wasn't even counting post-secondary. Every advantage in the world, short of my folks being literal billionaires. And it still wasn't enough to make me worth anything. I still had to cheat. Still had to steal to get where I am. Where I used to be, more like, because now I have sweet fuck all. And all of it is my fault.

My brain does that thing it sometimes does when things are too fucking much, severing the part of me that sees myself from the rest of me. Now I'm looking down at this wrecked, quivering, ugly blob that used to think he was a man, my ghostly stomach churning with disgust as he snivels into his lap, curled up on a therapist's couch like a little bitch.

That's me. That will always be me, no matter how brave a face I put on. Inside me there'll always be this come-stain on the rug, this meaningless sack of shit, blubbering like a sissy about having to take responsibility for his actions. As if that was choice. As if running away was ever a choice.

Every mistake I've ever made is ground so deep into my being that there is no such thing as running away, no such thing as freedom from the fuck-up that is me, the fire I've made of my life. Every mistake is an admission that I'm not worth a damn, that my father is right and I can't be trusted to live up to his standards.

Standards that turned me into this.

It ends, this freak out, this meltdown, this whatever I'm meant to call it. It ends and leaves me curled up on my side on Dr. Whitman's leather couch. He's turned down the lights and started playing music, a slow drone of soft sound without words or even a tune that swells and falls like waves on a sunny shore. The glass of water on the table in front of me gleams in the hazy light, and I concentrate on it, on unkinking my body enough that I can sit up and drink it.

"How long was I gone for?" I croak, clutching the empty glass in both hands.

"Only a few minutes. Do you have many panic attacks?"

"Is that what that was?" Whitman's face stills. I've surprised him again. "Not as often as I used to."

"What used to cause them?" he asks as I unbend my arms to put the glass on the table.

"Him. Thinking about what he was going to say when he found out how I fucked up."

There was always something I could have done better. A bonus question I should have gotten right, an award I might have earned that some other kid edged me out on. I swallow hard, my mouth sticky even though I just slammed that glass of water. Whitman fills the glass again and I drink, trying not to gulp it too quickly, my stomach feeling the stretch.

"I got grounded once because I had a pen mark on my school shirt," I say out of nowhere, staring into the glass, too burnt to raise my head. "He took my phone away for a week. It was the only thing I had left to take. He'd already taken the PlayStation. My TV. He would have boarded up my bedroom windows if he could have got away with it. Keep me from being distracted by, I don't know, air and shit."

"Do you see your father often?"

"Not if I can help it. Maybe that's why I don't have as many panic attacks these days."

A soft chime rings and Dr. Whitman closes his notebook. "We're going to have to end there, I'm afraid. If you're still feeling dysregulated, you're welcome to sit in the waiting room for a few minutes before you have to face the world."

More psych words, but every industry has its lingo, its catchphrases. Dysregulated is right, my head feeling like it's on backwards, my stomach churning even though all that's in there is water. Nothing I haven't dealt with before. I've run track meets after an attack. If I tried to bail, he only got worse.

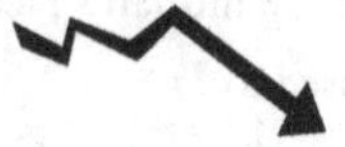

Another few sessions with Whitman and I start to see how the things that happened in my childhood have locked me into these self-destructive behavior patterns. The sort of hippy woo sentence that used to make me gag, but it's a fair trade to get choked by Carter's dick again.

In the meanwhile, I don't text him. That doesn't make sense unless I explain what an effort it is every day not to send him a message. Just a *hi*, a *wyd*, anything. But Whitman thinks I need to give him time. Work on myself a bit more, instead of rushing into a relationship I'm not ready to contribute to. Delayed gratification, and it's fucking brutal. Like edging myself all day long, my phone sitting in my pocket like a lit firecracker, every notification making me jump. So when Carter texts me suddenly a couple weeks after we met, I don't know how to reply:

Haven't heard from you lately, hope things are alright. HMU if you need to.

Hit him up for what? Money, advice, a job reference? He's the one who said to stop telling him stuff about me. I compose six replies and delete them all. I'm either too mean or too much of a simp, so in the end I just write, *im cool thx 4 asking,* and send it before I change my mind.

A couple days later he does it again. I reply just as briefly, but it's nice to know he hasn't written me off. That he still gives a shit. Have I made a real friend?

It's not like I have no friends, but they're all ballers like Mitch, burning through cash to live the life of their dreams before it's too late. Not one of them has been in touch since I posted about leaving Paladin. It's not like we were blood brothers, but it stings to know that I'm disposable.

Whitman talks me through that one too. I don't know what I'm going to do when I run out of money. I've applied for more than thirty positions, everything I'm remotely qualified for, but I can't even get an interview. I wouldn't be surprised if Ajay put me on blast and turned the whole sector against me.

Meanwhile, Carter slowly opens up. He claims that he's happy being a bartender, and while before I might have laughed at him for settling for so little, I've seen enough bars on a busy night, the way drinks are priced so that no one asks for change, the way they offer 18% as the lowest tip option on the card reader. I used to pick 'custom' and tip ten percent and feel like a fucking genius. I would have shorted Carter.

Six more sessions and another panic attack later—I used to think they were aneurysms; the MRI crew at St. Joseph's know me by sight—Whitman and I agree that I can see Carter again. I don't know what will happen, whether we'll go on an actual date or if I'll just beg him to come over and...

I shouldn't think too hard about that while I'm writing the text, which I keep deleting and starting again. I'm such a fucking simp for this guy and I don't even know if he'll give me anything in return.

so I'm in therapy

I put my phone down on my bed and go to the kitchen, where I down a can of kombucha drink like it's a Red Bull shot. It tastes like ass and not an ass I want to eat, but I'm trying to kick the energy drinks, which Whitman suggested were making my anxiety worse. Right now I'm shaking like I'm six cans deep, like asking Carter if he'll see me is the most important question I'll ever ask.

When I come back to my phone he's replied: *good to know*
c me?
ok when's good for you?

Now. Right now. Come and give me what I want. Put me on my knees and wreck me. Am I really that big a slut, that all I can think of is getting railed? But isn't that what we want from each other? So I shoot my shot, like so many guys. Saying the absolute least because I don't know what else to say.

   wydrn?

He replies with a laughing emoji. And for a moment I think about telling him to eat the biggest bag of dicks, then erasing his number from my phone and never thinking about him ever again. Like that would work. Like I'm not a desperate little bitch. I just know I'd spend the rest of my pathetic life dipping in and out of every bar in Toronto, trying to hunt him down. So when I get his next reply it's like a stay of execution.

   I can stop by for a little before work
   ok thx
   do you actually have a bed?
   y
   See? Pathetic.

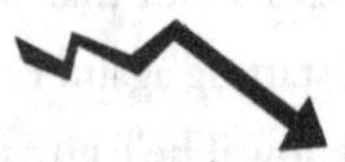

Carter shows up dressed for bar work in dark jeans and a band t-shirt, a canvas bag over his shoulder, cheap sunglasses perched on his head. While I sit on the bed and blab about intergenerational trauma he drifts about my bedroom inspecting what few things I have left: a steel coffee mug, a box of tissues, a luxury fashion magazine I picked up off from a pile someone left on the little wall fronting their property. People in Toronto are always leaving out their trash like this and I'd never once thought to pick anything up, but that picture of Cilian Murphy on the cover was too good to pass up. He flips through a few pages, making a face when he finds the ones that are stuck together, then tosses it on the end of the bed.

"You don't have to tell me everything, you know," he says, crossing his arms as he leans one shoulder against the wall. "That's your personal business."

"I thought you'd want to know how far I've come."

"I'm proud that you went for it." Something in his smile makes me feel hot and cold at the same time. "Are you alright?" he asks with a worried crease between his dark brows.

"Yeah. I'm cool. I just didn't get a lot of that, growing up. It feels weird to hear it."

"To hear that someone's proud of you? Daddy issues much?"

"Loads."

Is it the crack in my voice or the look in my eyes that tips him off, that betrays how he's affecting me? I don't know and I don't care as he shoves off the wall and moves towards me slowly.

"Are you saying you're looking for someone to command you, then praise you when you're good?" he asks, a heat igniting in his fathomless eyes. I try to reply but I can't fucking breathe so I nod. He laughs and for once I don't care as he stops at the edge of the bed, his belt buckle level with my eyes.

"He spank you much?" he asks as I look up at him.

"He barely even looked at me," I whisper, because all of a sudden I'm shaking too hard to breathe, the room spinning around me. Then Carter puts his hand on the top of my head and it's like I'm coming up for air, like his heavy touch made me real again. "What the fuck did you just do to me?"

"Tested one of your boundaries, it looks like."

"I didn't mean to freak out."

"No one means to freak out," he says gently as he starts to pet my head. "It'd be great if self-discovery was a linear process, but sometimes trauma sneaks up on you."

"This has nothing to do with my trauma."

"Being ignored by your parents is a form of abuse."

"They weren't cruel. They were just busy. They...I shouldn't tell you my personal business, should I?"

"Right now you can, if it's going to help you process this."

"I don't want to process anything. I just wanted to see you."

"You don't get one without the other, Reagan. I'm not sinking to your level. You have to rise to meet mine."

I will. I want to. Help me. Teach me. Save me. Never leave me. I don't care if that makes me a simp, I can't handle it if he walks away now. I need him, need his strength, his confidence, his indifference. I need someone who wants nothing from me, because nothing is all I have. All things I should be saying out loud but can't, my throat closing as my heart accelerates. Carter's expression softens as he slips his hand down to cradle my chin.

"My poor little people pleaser," he murmurs, tightening his grip when I try to look away. "Is that what you want? To please me?"

I nod against the pressure of his grip under my jaw. I'll do whatever he tells me if it means he doesn't leave. Let him have me anyway he wants, because even in this desperation, I've never felt so fucking alive. Nothing touches this moment, not the first time I had sex, my first split stock, that Lambo I drove at the racetrack, and all he's doing is holding my chin as he looks into my eyes, a hungry smile spreading across his gorgeous lips.

"I'll bet you want to know what that feels like, pleasing me," he says in that same velvet murmur that strokes down my spine. I nod again, my hips twitching with stoked up desire as he lets go of my chin and steps back.

"Hands and knees, Reagan," he says, a deep timbre in his voice I haven't heard before. My mouth watering, my dick leaking, my whole body electrified, I fall over myself trying to get into position kneeling on the bed where he points.

"Good boy," he purrs, and though I shouldn't care, shouldn't want to be spoken to like a dog, I can't contain the desperate whimper that creeps from between my lips as he puts his hand on the small of my back.

"Are you going to spank me?" I blurt as he squeezes my ass cheek.

"Do you want me to?"

"Am I supposed to know the answer?"

"It would help," he says, chuckling.

"Okay. Yes. Go for it."

"Seeing as we're still getting to know each other, I'll let you keep your clothes on."

"What should I do?"

"Stay."

As he walks away I bite my tongue. I'm not a dog. Except I am. A drooling, shaking, wordless animal waiting for its master, and though I shouldn't be ashamed, though Dr. Whitman and everything I've read tells me that all kinds of sex are okay as long as everyone consents, I can't hide my shaking or the hot blush up the back of my neck.

"What's your safe word," he asks from some unknown distance.

"I don't know."

"Do you know red-yellow-green light?"

"Like for driving?"

"No, for giving consent, so I know how much farther I can take you."

"Dude, what are you planning to do to me?"

"It doesn't matter what I'm doing. You get to set your own limits, no matter what we decide in advance."

"So it's green for go, red for stop, yellow for..."

"For let's dial it back or switch to some other kind of play."

"Alright. I get it."

"Don't worry. I'll take it easy on you."

I'm about to tell him not to bother when he hits me. Not that hard, as I found out later, but swiftly and sharply, smacking my ass with the rolled up fashion magazine.

"How was that?" he asks, rubbing his other hand over the sore spot.

"I don't have much to compare it to," I say, my tense voice betraying my surprise.

"I like the way it makes your ass jerk."

"Then you should do it again."

He does, the hot pain flaring across both my ass cheeks. Another, and maybe this one was harder or maybe I just don't like it but I cry out sharply.

"Talk to me, Reagan."

"Yellow," I gasp as he presses the flat of his hand against the hot throbbing.

"Good boy," he hums. "You don't have to ever worry about disappointing me by saying no, Reagan. I want you to want this too. What makes me happy is knowing that I'm driving you wild, that I'm making you want me more and more."

As he talks he strokes my tingling ass, dipping his fingers between my thighs to graze against my balls then up again between my cheeks. Touching me through my clothes and it's the hottest thing that's ever happened to me, my dick leaking into my pants as I push back against his touch. And then he lifts his hand, leaving me shaking.

"That's enough for now," he says, tossing the magazine on the bed.

"But—"

"I gotta go to work," he says with a laugh as he sits beside me. He sets his hand on the back of my neck, a hot, steadying weight. "I'll call you soon. I've got back to back shifts but then I get a few days off, we can go for dinner. I'll pay."

"Are you sure? I'm not totally broke."

"Keep your money, Reagan. You need it more than I do. Speaking of, are you still planning to give this place up?

"I have to. I'm burning through cash."

"If you get stuck for somewhere to stay, there's room at our place."

"I thought you were single."

"I am. It's a shared house."

"You don't have your own place?"

"In this economy? I mean, if our spare room's no good you could always move back in with your parents."

"Yeah, right. That'll fix my daddy issues." *If I have to move back in with that asshole, one of us won't be making it out alive.*

THE STRAY

KARL

Do you have that one friend who seems so relaxed, so chill, who every now and then does something unhinged? Gets a tattoo sleeve or quits his job, starts a cult in Guadeloupe? Carter is one such friend. Most often he has bad sex with someone he doesn't like. This feels different, his covert relationship with this Reagan person, about who I have heard so little they might be a woman for all I know. Unlikely, but Carter rarely speaks of them. Only speaks *to* them by text message several times a day, every day for the last six weeks or so.

What can I say to my friend, however? I have made similar abrupt choices, overturned my whole life in a single decision. Like when I came out as bi to my boyfriend. He gave me such a look of disgust that I nearly took it back. Pretended it wasn't true. I chose myself instead of him, and while that was good for my soul, it was a disaster for my life.

When I told Carter that Zander had kicked me out, he didn't hesitate. Yes, he likes having help to pay the rent, but I know he would have offered his spare room to me even if not. And I am not so proud that I will refuse such gifts from my friends.

Let's be honest, we all take what we can get. I happily stuffed this free Toronto Public Library tote bag with a few leftover copies of the books from tonight's launch. Not to sell even though they're signed, because the author's work deserves respect, but to give as gifts throughout the year, a convenience that keeps me from having to dig into my pocket. Only a little cheat, you see? I'm really a very good person.

So when I see the strange man huddling in the corner of the porch, drenched by the rain that had conveniently stopped by the time I got out of the subway, my first thought is not to threaten him but to give him a chance to speak first. His collared shirt is plastered to his skin, the rain trickling down his forehead and leaving a slick of hair product.

"D-d-d-do you know C-c-c-carter?" he stammers, clutching his arms.

"I do."

"D-d-d-did he say anything about R-r-reagan?"

"That is you?"

He nods, little droplets flying from his hair. "He s-s-said you maybe had a room I could c-c-crash in. If things got fucked up."

"It looks like things are very fucked up. Carter will be working late but you can come in with me. I don't bite."

He flinches back, his eyes wide, and for a heartbeat I hate Carter very much, because this Reagan is delightful to look at, with sweetly pink lips that pout just so and a lithe little body beneath that clinging shirt. This will not be the first time that Carter got in first. Men of my size get too often overlooked by these fit young gays, but that's not something I feel the need to change. They can take me or leave me.

Reagan I leave dripping on the doormat while I get a towel for him. "You can have a shower to warm up," I tell him. "We will have clothes you can borrow."

"Where are you from?" he asks as he dabs his hair with the towel.

"Zupanja. We left Croatia after the war."

"There was a war?"

"There is always a war." I could go on and on, until this young man could bathe in his tears, but I won't. Not everyone deserves to know what it cost me to survive. Even if they are fucking my roommate.

I lend him a sweatshirt and that one pair of underwear I paid too much for and so cannot throw away even though they will always be too small. As I make myself a snack to soak up the complimentary book launch wine, Reagan huddles on the couch thumbing through his phone, his knees tucked up under the sweatshirt. As I lean out the kitchen doorway to ask if he's hungry as well, he settles into the couch deeper, my sweatshirt riding up to bare the pink curve of the back of his thigh.

Perhaps I am not as good a person as I want to think. As I wait for the microwave to warm last night's leftovers, I keep making reasons to look at him, this young man of Carter's. It's not only his thigh that attracts me. I have a weakness for strays, used to torment my mother by trying to claim every cat that wandered through our yard. Zander was a stray, five years younger than me and so willing, so sweet when we met, all lips and hips but no confidence. Until I disturbed his imagination with the facts.

I turn and Reagan is standing in the doorway. I need to find this boy some pants very soon, to cover those muscled legs of his. He's sculpted his damp hair into a little pompadour, the stretched collar of my old sweatshirt drooping around his collarbones and if he wasn't Carter's I would...

"Do you need something?" I ask, to stop myself from thinking about what I would do to him if he were mine.

"I wanted to charge my phone." He holds up a new iPhone.

"The whole house is Android. But I think someone left a Mac charger when they stayed. In that drawer beside you."

As he rummages through the take-out cutlery, rubber bands, and other debris in the hide-everything drawer, I get myself some water, a fork, the block of parmesan and the cheese grater. Yes, it's more complicated, but my Italian grandmother will rise from the grave if I dare to use that pulverized American cheese dust on her ragù recipe.

"Smells good," he says.

"Are you hungry?"

"I'm okay."

"There's plenty. More than I need to be eating at this hour."

"I'm fine."

I don't want to make him uncomfortable, so I leave him to his search and take my plate out to the sitting room. Briefly I think about clearing a space on our table amid the piles of books, game cases, and other things we let build up, but it's far easier to take my usual place on the couch.

Muttering to himself in the kitchen, Reagan closes the drawer with a bang, then wanders out to the sitting room, where he drops onto the other end of the couch. He glances my way then sits up, pulling the sweatshirt down his hips.

"So you're his roommate?" he asks, his eyes wandering over me as I set my plate on the coffee table.

"I am. My name is Karl. Does Carter know you were coming?"

He shakes his head, not meeting my gaze. "Has he said much about me?" he asks, his voice graveled, his fair cheeks turning rose before my eyes.

"A little. You lost your job, right?"

"And my condo. Though really I gave it up. The manager said I could get my last month's rent back if I left early. I guess they have a waiting list. I didn't know the rental market was so tight."

"You gave up your lease without having a new one? That's brave."

"It was stupid. Now I'm out of options. No one wants an unemployed loser."

"Don't call yourself a loser. You are a man with difficulties."

"No, I'm pretty sure I'm a loser. Let me have this one, dude. I deserve everything that's happened." He presses his lips together, his eyes gleaming with tears he won't shed in front of me, the proud little man.

"How long do you have?" I ask.

"Two days."

"Shit. That's bad."

"I know."

"We have a spare room. It isn't much. And you would need to empty it."

"I don't want to be in your way."

"We can accommodate you for a little time. I don't think Carter would allow me to refuse."

"Can he do that?"

"It was his apartment first. He rescued me. Like this. I couldn't stay where I was, so he let me stay here. I liked it so much—we both liked it—that I never left."

"I'll only be here a couple days. I'll either get a job or an apartment, and then I won't be your problem."

"As you need. Once I've eaten, I'll help you clean the room."

Carter and I have debated the origin of this skinny room slotted between the kitchen and bathroom. A pantry? A toilet? A maid's bedroom? An attempt to divide a larger room in two? It's barely wider than the old sash window in the wall opposite the door, with just enough space for a futon we never lay flat, and the pile of shipping boxes and winter clothes that lives on top of it. Reagan asks no questions as we sort everything, his bare legs flashing when he bends over, his ass problematic. Only if I make it a problem. I am, after all, a very good person at heart. I can enjoy Carter's happiness without resenting either of them.

Perched on the edge of the bare futon, his knees together, his head down, Reagan looks so very young and fragile. "Thanks for this," he mumbles. "Without you I'd be homeless soon."

"You are homeless."

His head snaps up. "What do you mean? I mean I'm here, aren't I?"

"Yes, but this isn't *your* home. Not every unhoused person is sleeping on the sewer grates. Many of us depended on the kindness of their friends and family or sometimes strangers who offer us a temporary solution."

"You mean *you* were homeless?"

"In so many words. My boyfriend of many years drove me out of our house in the middle of the night. I had nowhere else to go."

"So is Carter like the humane society or something?"

"Could be," I say, laughing at the mental picture of Carter swarmed by stray dogs, sobering as I remember that I am one of those dogs. I fetch a pillow and a sleeping bag for Reagan, who is still sitting on the futon when I come back.

"I always thought of *homeless* as being some guy with a squeegee and no teeth," he says as I set them down.

"That could easily be any one of us."

"I'm not going to end up like that."

"Let's hope not."

"I mean it. This is just temporary. I'll get back on top, you'll see." At a noise he springs to his feet. "Is that Carter?"

"Must be."

But he's already gone. I stay, wishing I did not slightly hate my best friend.

QUID PRO QUO

REAGAN

I MUST BE GETTING better at thinking before I speak, because I've gone over an hour without asking Carter's roommate to let me suck his dick. Like all it took was that one time to unlock something in me, some existential craving on the same level as food and shelter. Not that every man I see has affected me like this. Just Carter, and now Karl, who looks scarily like that one counselor at summer camp, the only year I was allowed to go.

Lee was the coolest adult I had ever met, with tattooed legs and a long beard he kept tied up in elastics, like the thing on King Tut's chin. He was into death metal and played Magic the Gathering and I'm pretty sure he was my first gay crush, until night came and he told a ghost story so brutally realistic that I didn't sleep again until my parents came to get me.

This is what happens when you raise kids without an imagination.

Karl has the same bearish build, the same gingerish beard though it's expertly trimmed, the same gruff energy as Lee, and it's fucking with my head. So much that I almost jump Carter as he opens the door.

He stops in the doorway, blinking at me. "Why are you naked?" he grunts.

"My clothes got wet. And hello? How am I naked?" I pluck at Karl's huge sweatshirt, which comes halfway down my thighs.

"Where are your pants?"

"Hung in the shower to dry," Karl says, joining us. "Poor thing was soaked to the bone."

"Why is he even here?" Carter asks him.

"I gave up the condo," I say as he kicks off his shoes.

He frowns at me. "For good? That was fast."

"I needed the money."

"Let me guess," he says with a smirk. "You didn't count on how hard it is to find a vacancy in this city."

"I told him our spare room is his as long as he needs it," Karl says quietly, lingering in the doorway to the living room, his hands in the pockets of his linen trousers. Who the fuck wears linen trousers on a Wednesday? My new crush, that's who.

As Karl (the new crush) follows Carter (the original crush, crush 2.0 of my newly redesigned libido) into the kitchen, I sneak away to my little room. I've stayed in places smaller than this—in New York, in Tokyo—but only for a night or two. The thought that I might spend the next month, the next year in a room so small I can almost touch both walls at once feels a bit like facing jail.

Bullshit. I'm a little bitch if I think there's any comparison. Jail would have fucked me up. I'm too short, too angry, too quick to lash out. Losing everything was worth the cost. At least I have my freedom.

And nothing else. I still haven't told my parents I got fired. If I'm lucky, I won't ever have to.

Huddled on the futon, I pull my knees up to my chin, wrapping the sleeping bag around me. The rain has started again, drops oozing down the darkened window and probably leaking through the roof of the old house. I got excited when I first saw the place this afternoon, though I was curious how a bartender could carry the mortgage on a semidetached West End brick Victorian. Of course he's just renting one of the upper floor apartments. Of course he has a roommate. A burly, bearish roommate with sparkling blue eyes and a great big heart who I absolutely cannot bang.

I can hear them talking in the living room. I should stop hiding in my room like a chickenshit, get out there and show my face. See how dry my jeans are, so Carter stops glaring at me like he caught me getting railed over the back of the couch. I should stop thinking about getting railed by anyone over anything until I sort out my shit. As I shrug off the sleeping bag and get to my feet their voices grow louder, like they're approaching my door.

"So you aren't sleeping with him?" Karl asks in that husky accent that makes him twice as interesting.

"Why, do you want a piece?"

Karl makes a noncommittal noise. "I wouldn't kick him out of bed."

I should pretend I didn't hear that. I shouldn't even be listening. I am very bad at following orders, especially my own, as I carefully creep closer to the door.

"He's...well, he's not the easiest to get along with," Carter says.

"It sounds like he's going through a rough time."

"Please. He's a walking advertisement for regulatory intervention."

"But are you sleeping with him?" he asks with a chuckle.

"No," Carter replies as if it's obvious. "Don't you remember, he's the guy who sucked me off at the rec center."

"I know."

"So?"

"So...what?"

"You know, I don't want to talk about it right now. It was a slow night, I didn't make jack shit for tips, and I feel like trash."

"I wondered why you're home early."

"We'll figure everything out tomorrow," Carter says through a yawn.

"Of course. Sleep well."

"You too," he replies from further away. A door closes, and then another, and that's it. I've survived one more day.

Surviving the night is much harder. I normally have to stream a movie or some shows to fall asleep, but I never found a cable to charge my iPhone and I'm saving my data for emergencies. Lately every day feels like an emergency.

Lying on the lumpy futon listening to the rain trickle down a drainpipe outside the window, I try my best not to think about their conversation. Without success, because every time I close my eyes I see Carter standing over me. Feel his hand on my head, on the back of my neck. Taste his come, remembering the heat of it splashing on my cheek.

Weak...simp...beta... "Shut up," I hiss out loud to drown out the voices as I yank up Karl's sweatshirt, releasing another cloud of his unusual cologne. Groaning, trying not to, I wriggle his boxer briefs down my hips to free my hard-on. No one has to know. No one has to know how weak I am around these men, how many nights have already ended like this, with me biting my pillow or my arm to keep from shouting Carter's name. This isn't a crush, it's an epidemic, and I don't know if there's a cure.

There's only gasping moments of relief as I climax in record time, spilling onto my heaving stomach. A relief that fades in an instant as I realize I don't have any way to clean up. Somehow I manage to writhe out of Karl's sweatshirt without smearing it with come. Holding my sticky hand out of the way, my jocks halfway down my thighs, I open my door a crack, but the apartment is dark. In the narrow, musty bathroom I wash my hand and junk, then use someone's mouthwash in lieu of brushing my teeth. Tomorrow I'll pick up what's left at the condo, then hand over my keys as a sign of good faith. Maybe the property manager Alison will let me use her as a reference. Or maybe she'll tell me to get fucked after all my complaints of the last year and a half.

Is there a bridge I haven't burned? This one, so I better be on my best behavior to not make Carter regret his offer. A noble thought, but I can't ignore the ache in my empty stomach. I haven't eaten all day, too busy and then too conscious of the cost, and then too rained on. Karl did offer me food, so I creep to the kitchen and poke about in their ancient fridge until I find some vegan yogurt (yikes), the only thing that doesn't need to be cooked. I take a few walnuts from a jar on the counter, and I'm sorting through the unmatched cutlery in the dish drainer for a spoon when I feel the hair on the back of my neck rise. I turn to find Carter yawning in the doorway.

"Karl said I could help myself," I say, not strictly true but it seems to satisfy Carter, who nods then opens the fridge. "You know you can fuck me if you want to. It's only fair."

Sighing, he closes the fridge then turns to me. "Look, Reagan, you're hot, and you're obviously down to fuck, but has no one ever been nice to you?"

"Like how?"

"I didn't offer you somewhere to stay because I want something from you. I just wanted to help."

"And I want to show you that I appreciate it."

"Dude, it's not a quid pro quo," he groans. "You don't owe me anything."

"But what if I wanted to?"

"Then it should be because you want it, not because you think I expect payment. I'm just trying to be a decent person."

He's right. He's right and I'm a whore. Creeping around in his kitchen naked except for another man's underpants, trying to trade my ass for a vegan yogurt and half a dozen walnuts.

"You've clearly drunk the Kool-Aid," he says more gently when I can't answer. "You bought into the capitalist lie. It's not hard to do, but we're not all hustling all the time. Some of us are trying to be good to each other. So please don't feel that you owe me anything."

"But if I wanted to…"

He shakes his head. "I still don't think this is the right time to take that step in our relationship."

"Woah, who said this is a relationship?"

"Me. All human interaction is a relationship. Whether we fuck or not is just a variable in that relationship."

"Okay, but will we ever?"

"Not while you're so dependent on me. What happens if we have a fight? You don't live here. I could tell you to leave at any time."

"You wouldn't do that."

"You don't know that. I'm not trying to scare you, Reagan, but we can't bring sex into this right now. Or at least we shouldn't."

He's right. Again, but as I try to slip past him he bars me with his arm. "Hey, it's okay," he murmurs, cupping my chin when I try to look away. "I'm not saying no. I'm just saying not now."

"But soon?"

"Greedy, aren't you?"

"What gave it away?"

"This," he murmurs, brushing his thumb across my lips. Expecting—craving—a kiss, I open my mouth, but instead he rests his forehead against mine, his hand tensing on my jaw when I try to turn my head and get my mouth on his.

"Easy does it," he breathes in that laughing tone. "If it's worth it, it's worth waiting for."

TEMPTATION

KARL

I WAS SURE I would get used to Reagan after a few days. Two and a half weeks later, he has risen to the top of the chart for most frustrating person alive.

Because I want him. Pathetically, the way I used to want Viggo Morgenstern to scoop me up and bear me away. Religiously, jerking off in the shower every night after work to make it through another evening with Reagan hovering at the periphery of my vision, curled up in the monstrous old armchair that the previous tenants had left, possibly as they couldn't get it through the front door.

I thought he was being proud when he told me he didn't need help moving in, until he returned an hour later with everything he owned in the world in a pair of cardboard boxes and a Gucci duffle bag. Since then he's done what he could to find work and another apartment, but he is, as they say, punching above his weight, looking for a job at a similar salary to the one he lost. Chances are, his old employer spread the word that he'd been let go. He needs to think about taking what he can get. But that's not my place to say. Reagan is young, but he is no child. And even children must be allowed to learn through failure.

He has much to learn.

On Sunday we—Carter and I—meet up with our long-time friend Baldwin. He and Carter met on a gay men's football (don't you dare call it soccer) league, discovering one night after a savage defeat and several rounds at the pub that they knew all the same people in Toronto's goth/queer/kink scenes. Late night pizza after events at the Velvet Underground turned into meeting for dinner before clubbing, to meeting just for dinner, then brunch shortly after I moved in.

We're finishing our meal when Carter's phone buzzes. We try to not check our messages while we eat, so he glances at us for agreement then turns over his phone and thumbs the unlock screen. He watches whatever it is for a few seconds then groans, letting his hand drop onto the table. The video keeps playing, of Reagan wearing that cropped Care Bears t-shirt he bought last week from some Parkdale vintage dealer and those tiny green running shorts of his as he dances around our sitting room with the mop.

"Who's the snack?" Wyn asks, craning his neck to watch as it replays.

"Reagan. He lost his apartment so I said he could crash with us for a little."

"How much longer is he staying?" I ask.

"Are you guys not getting along?" Carter says, pocketing his phone.

"That's not the problem."

"Then what is?"

I glance at Wyn, who is studiously stirring his coffee. "Is Reagan at all aware of how he acts?"

"What do you mean?"

"Like he's a cam boy on a non-stop livestream. I'm on a work call and he's prancing up and down outside my room, dusting the ceiling in one of those little outfits he keeps buying though he says he has no money."

"Maybe he wants you to fuck him," Carter says gruffly.

"You mean you two aren't…" Wyn says to him, frowning as he searches for the right word.

"We aren't anything," Carter replies. "We basically went from him blowing me in public to him dressing like a snack in my apartment."

"I'm sorry, what?" Wyn says, twisting in his seat to gape at him. "You didn't tell me any of that."

"It's not my story to tell," I say as Carter turns to me with a pained expression.

"Fine," he sighs. "Coles' notes version, I met this younger man out in the wild."

"Like, up the Bruce?" Wyn asks, frowning.

"Try Trinity Bellwoods Park," I say, trying not to laugh.

"Is this or is this not my story to tell?" Carter says with a cross look. "Point is, we fooled around and he left his wallet behind. When we met up so I could give it back, he told me how fucked up things were for him, so I offered for him to crash at our place if he was stuck for somewhere to stay. But we're not dating or hooking up or anything, okay?"

"Do I get to meet him?" Baldwin asks after a stilted moment.

"Why would you want to?"

"Why not?"

"Maybe because he's a libertarian?" I suggest.

Wyn twists to face our friend again. "Yo, Carter…you're fucking a libertarian?"

"This isn't about me. And I just told you, I'm not fucking him."

"Yet," Wyn said with a smirk.

"The hell it isn't," I say at the same time. "How isn't this about you?"

"Because he's just a person. I would have done the same for anyone. And you can bet he's getting a taste of the dark side of economic rationalism, scrubbing our toilets."

"Sucking your dick," I mutter, and when did I become a bitch?

Carter drops his fork with a clatter. "What the fuck, dude?"

"You tell me, you're the one sleeping with Ayn Rand. I wouldn't blame you," I go on as Carter groans and drops his head in his hands. "He's a real *red* hot piece of ass."

"You want him that bad?" he snarls, shoving back from the table. "Be my fucking guest." He stands up, whips a fifty from his wallet, throws it on the table, then marches away.

"So what are you going to do?" Wyn asks as I pick the banknote out of the puddle of ketchup on Carter's plate.

"What would you do?"

"Keep my damn mouth shut."

EVICTED

REAGAN

I'VE NEVER WORKED THIS hard in my life. Sure, I used to go all night playing the Tokyo exchange, then switch straight into my work deck and keep going, fueled by sugar-free energy drinks, Adderall, and arrogance. Time stops existing in that state, becoming just another scrolling ticker on the screen, a set of iterating digits that limit your trading windows and have no connection to real life. But doing sixteen hours in a chair designed to make your ass feel weightless isn't that hard compared to cleaning this fucking house.

The apartment isn't even the whole house, just a bunch of upstairs rooms, but everywhere I turn there's something else covered in dust, or grease, or that nasty finger dirt that builds up on the doorframes.

The guys aren't messy as far as guys go, but I've never lived anywhere that didn't come with a housekeeper. My parents always had Martha, and now use Martha's daughter Brittney. Even in the condo, I paid a Jamaican woman to come in once a week to scrub my shit off the toilet and vacuum my epithelial cells off the windowsills and countertops and floors.

I should have been paying her more.

Some parts of this old house are uncleanable, the dirt so ingrained, the surfaces so fragile that scrubbing does more harm than good. But it's exercise, and a way to pay the guys back for letting me stay with them. Even if Carter keeps telling me I don't owe him anything.

What's an even bigger pain in the ass than scraping his fingerprints off the light switches is trying to find a new job. A few days ago I sucked it up and texted Ajay to ask if he'd mentioned my firing to anyone. He replied instantly with *I had to sorry but it's a matter of ethics*. And then blocked me.

With Carter and Karl both out of the house at their weekly brunch meet-up, I can sweep and then mop the whole apartment in one go. Aside from their rooms, which I never go into, because I'm not a psycho. Waiting for the hallway to dry so I can hit the kitchen, I make another of my stupid little videos, singing into the mop handle as I show off my tragic shuffle dance from grade school. Carter can't hate my reels too much, seeing that he keeps replying to them, usually with a lol emoji, now and then a face palm.

Maybe there's a future for me on TikTok. I'm daydreaming of names for my channel as I put away the mop and stuff when Carter flings open the front door.

"What the fuck are you doing?" he says, slamming it behind him.

"Doesn't this stuff go in the hall closet?"

"I don't mean the fucking mop," he hisses. "What's with all these videos?"

"I won't send you any more if you don't like them."

"Why are you making them in the first place?"

"Because I'm bored."

His dark eyes flare hot as he looks me over. "Who else are you sending them to?"

"Excuse me?"

"You heard me." He wrenches himself around and stomps away down the hall.

"Hey! Take off your shoes. I just washed that."

He turns on his heel, his face flushed, his hands clenched. Just as suddenly he pivots away and carries on towards his room.

"What did I even do?" I call after him, but if he answers it's lost in the slam of his bedroom door.

I cram the bucket and other crap in the overflowing hall closet then go wash my hands. Slowly, because I'm totally confused. What does he think I'm trying to do? The closet's shitty door has popped open by the time I'm done, and I'm restacking the shoes in the bottom when Carter comes raging up the hall again.

"So what's the deal with Karl?" he spits, his hands on his hips.

"Deal? I don't have a deal with him."

"You don't think there's something sus about all this?" he says, gesturing to my outfit as I get to my feet.

"So? Housework makes me hot. And I'm trying to, you know, embrace the lifestyle."

"Coming out as gay doesn't mean you have to become a slut."

I step back like he took a swing at me. "Excuse the fuck me? Are you high? The last person I did anything with was you, dickhead."

"How long until you fuck Karl?"

Is he for real? "Is that what this is? You're going to get mad at me for cheating on you when a, we're not dating and b, I haven't even done it yet?"

"Yet," he says through his teeth. One syllable that breaks everything between us.

"You know what, Carter, fuck you. What even is your problem?"

"I didn't use to have any problems," he snarls. "Then I let your dumb ass make me act like an even bigger dumbass and now I'm fucking stuck with you."

"Wow. So you want me to leave?"

"Yep. In fact, why don't you do that? Right now." Grinning horribly, he yanks open the door. "Go on, Mr Pull-yourself-up-by-your-bootstraps, last of the self-made men. Go out there and get what you deserve from life."

"But—"

"Get out!"

I do, because he's terrifying, spittle flying from his lips, all kindness gone from his eyes. I do, because it's what he wants, even if it's killing me to shove my bare feet into my stupid fifteen hundred dollar shoes and step through that open door. Which he slams behind me so suddenly it slaps my nearly naked ass.

Because I'm still wearing that crop top and those shorts. Dressed for a hot day at Pride, not for the rest of my life. I shiver, though the temperature's the same. My wallet, my phone, my everything in the world is inside that apartment. I was wrong before, when I thought I had nothing. That was luxury. This...this is a problem.

A big problem. Serious. Dangerous. My fault. My fault without even trying, my fault because the person with all the power decided that it was. My heart hammers at my ribs, my stomach knotting around what might be the last food I ever eat.

If you're reading this and thinking I'm overreacting, then you probably don't have anxiety. Your brain doesn't tell you that you're dying whenever someone rejects you. Maybe you'll be sad, or angry that they didn't give you a chance. Me, on the other hand? I feel like I'm having a heart attack, my limbs numb where they aren't tingling, my head throbbing, my stomach trying hard to turn itself inside out in both directions.

Deep in the mix, I know it's a lie, that this isn't a heart attack but a symptom of my mental illness. Yet on the surface, all I can think is that I'm going to die on Carter's landing because I can't even call 9-1-1 because my phone is behind this door, as is my whole world.

By the time Karl gets home I'm numb, my panicky energy burned up, leaving me shaky and nauseous as I huddle in the corner of the stairwell. With his help I get to my feet, whimpering pathetically as his warmth bleeds into me.

"Did you lock yourself out?" he asks.

"He kicked me out," I whisper, my throat wrecked from choking back my sobs. "He thinks we're banging."

"You and I? Why would he think that?"

"I don't know," I squeak. "I've never done this before."

"Men and women aren't that different," he says with a fatherly smile.

"But I've never cared about anyone. Ever. And now I've pissed him off without even doing anything and—" I cover my mouth as my stomach threatens to empty. The ghost of eating disorders past, because puking was the quickest way to drop weight for the pole vault. Or the school dance. Or all the other reasons I invented in my pursuit of the perfect body weight.

"It's not like I've never dated or fucked anyone," I gulp, "but I never really gave a shit about them. They sure didn't care about me. Just in it for the money. But this isn't like that. I actually like Carter. Only now I've pissed him off without even doing anything and—"

"Hush, zečić," Karl says, putting his arm around my shoulder again. "He won't stay mad."

"What if he does?"

"Then he's missing out."

"On what?"

"On you. You won't be everyone's cup of tea. You may be some-one's shot of whiskey." He gives my shoulders another squeeze. "Stay here, and I'll see if I can't work something out."

"With Carter?"

"No, I think we will take him seriously. I have a friend who might be able to help you for a night or two, until I can talk Carter out of his jealousy."

He leaves me his corduroy blazer, which swamps me like his sweat-shirt but stops me from shivering. A couple minutes later he comes out with my Gucci weekender and said sweatshirt.

"No deal?" I ask as I swap it for his blazer.

"Wyn can put you up. As for Carter, give me a day. Maybe two."

"You're the boss."

He chuckles, though I can't imagine a single thing about this that's even slightly funny. As we come out of the building, the rideshare car waiting outside opens its trunk. Karl hands me my nearly empty bag.

"The car is paid for. But mind your manners. Wyn's doing you a favor."

"So are you. So if I don't see you again—"

"You will," he says firmly, resting both hands on my shoulders. "I promise." He dips his head and kisses me quickly on each cheek then claps my shoulders and steps back. I get into the back of the car and let it carry me away from the closest thing I have to a home.

RED FLAG

KARL

WHEN I COME BACK into the apartment Carter is angrily mowing down virtual zombies on the tv, so I take myself to my bedroom to figure out what I will say to him. A frustrating turn of events, as I'd hoped he and Reagan would get on with things, admit they are out of their minds for each other and start a proper relationship, so I could stop thinking about him.

Therefore I sent him to Baldwin's place for a night or two. If I comfort Reagan any harder, I'll give into his temptations, and I value Carter's friendship—and his second bedroom—too much to play those games. After an hour I'm no closer to knowing what to say, but I can't go on hiding in my room. Someone has to be the grown up.

"You sure don't waste time," Carter grunts as I walk past the sitting room.

"You're who kicked him out."

"Yeah, that might not have been the best idea."

"No shit."

He pauses the game and tosses the controller on the coffee table with a clunk. "Maybe not the worst idea if the first thing he did was run begging to you."

"I found him catatonic in the stairwell. What did you say to him?"

"Nothing."

"So he imagined you throwing him out? Did he also imagine you accusing him of trying to sleep with me?"

Chewing his lip, Carter can't answer, and good that he doesn't try, because what could he say? "What is there even between the two of you?" I ask, shoving my hands in my pockets to hide their trembling.

"I don't know. It's not like we're a couple. We fooled around once when we shouldn't have and that's it."

"So what are you so angry about? If the two of you aren't in an exclusive relationship, why do you even have a say?"

He glares at me, then crumbles, slumping forward with his elbows on his knees. "I don't know," he groans, rubbing the back of his neck. "Why the hell do I even care? He's such a red flag."

"He's young."

He sits up sharply. "I was never that dumb."

"No, I'm sure you were your own special brand of dumb. What is he, twenty-six? When I was that age, I still thought I was going to become the next Stephen King."

"You shouldn't put yourself down. Your books are awesome."

"My books are not the point. What I am trying to say is, you are enforcing boundaries on him that the two of you never discussed. You're mad because he is showing his body on the internet, but you have no claim on that body at all."

"Fuck. You're right. Okay, call him back in, I'm ready to apologize."

"He's not here. I sent him to Wyn's."

Frowning, he sucks in a breath, then just as quickly deflates. "I fucked this up pretty badly, didn't I?"

"Give him a night or two. Let him have a little vacation."

Carter rolls not merely his eyes but his whole head. "Yeah, he's really suffering, not having to work or pay rent."

"Remember, you are the only reason he isn't unhoused. He can't stay with his parents. He nearly went to jail. You're kicking him when he's down."

"Goddamn you and your moral compass." Sighing, he pushes his hands through his hair. "Why do I even care?"

"Because you're a compassionate person who sees the good in everyone. But you still have an ego, right? You still have feelings and all that messy stuff. Sometimes you're going to make bad choices. I say leave it for tonight. You'll both cool off, and we can talk about it tomorrow."

"What do you mean, *we*? I thought you weren't involved."

"I have to live with you assholes. If you aren't happy, none of us are happy."

Am I lying to Carter? If saying less than everything counts as a lie, then yes. I am lying by omission because I haven't told him that Reagan sends his flirty reels to me as well. I watch them late at night with my phone muted and my cock in my hand, because though I am a good person, there's not a person on earth who doesn't tell themselves that.

As Carter gets up from the couch to stretch, I go into the kitchen and fetch a glass of water (from the faucet, as I have never liked plastic bottles) then retreat to my bedroom. Before I get too comfortable. Before Reagan sends me another video. Before he causes any more friction between myself and my best friend.

Settled into a heap of pillows in the corner of my bed, I read the same page of the new T. Kingfisher novel five times before I accept that I can't concentrate. I trust Baldwin, whole heartedly. Trust him not to take advantage of someone inexperienced. Not to interfere in others' relationships.

But there is no relationship. Reagan is our houseguest and our friend. Carter doesn't want him, and I won't let myself have him. The fact that I can't stop thinking about him is my problem, not his. In reality, I have no claim on him at all. And I've just sent him into the mouth of temptation.

THE SNACK

WYN

THE SNACK ARRIVES IN a wide-body SUV that nearly scrapes the shit out of a door panel trying to reverse down the alley. I told the driver the only way out was to pull past my place and three-point in the other alley, but if he doesn't want to listen, that's not my fault. He wouldn't be the first to find out the hard way.

I watch from the front door until the SUV makes it back to Lansdowne without losing a mirror or damaging the siding on Niobe and Eric's house. Meanwhile Snack Boy—Reagan, though he looks more like a Braydon or Jaxon or Josh, with those frosted tips and that sporty build—peers around my apartment with a stunned expression, clutching his slick Gucci weekend bag under one arm.

"I hope the couch is good enough," I say as I shut the door. "This isn't the best set-up for guests."

"It's fine," he blurts, sounding so young I'm instantly ashamed that I've been sizing him up. He's fine though, in a twink sort of way. Not my type, but I can't stop staring at his pretty mouth as he compulsively licks his lips.

"Where do you sleep?" the lips ask.

"Upstairs. It's a loft."

"Then what's back there?" He nods towards the rear of the coach house. "It looked a lot bigger than this from the outside."

"Good spot. There is another room. My landlords live in the house up front. We cut a deal so they could leave some things back there."

"Why don't they get a storage unit?"

I can't keep from laughing. "It's stuff they need access to regularly. They wouldn't want to have to drive to a unit every time."

"What is it, gym equipment?"

Do I tell him? Does it matter? Karl said he and Carter had no claim on this kid, but that's a lot to throw at someone I've known for five minutes. Then he bends over to put his bag on the couch and that part in me that likes to eat little white twinks alive jumps up at the sight of those pink thighs under his baggy sweatshirt.

"It's a BDSM playroom."

He jerks upright, his eyes wide. "Wow. Really?"

"They rent it out as a homestay a few times a year. I clear out, get a hotel or go out of town."

"Isn't that a hassle?"

"Beats paying market rent. I don't even want to say out loud what I pay, it'll just piss you off." He's still staring over his shoulder at the gap between the ceiling and the top of the cupboards in the galley kitchen that marks the end of my half of the unit.

"You want to see it?" I ask.

"Is that cool with them?"

"Just don't break anything," I say as I fish the key to the sliding door out of the basket where they keep the homestay binder. I think my rent about covers the home equity loan my friends took out to reno their old garage into this place, which got a write up in the Toronto Star lifestyle section for its architecture.

That was before Eric and Niobe installed the St. Andrew's cross. And the sex swing. And the cage bed, which shocks people the most.

Reagan is no exception, gaping at the narrow cage of wrought iron bars beneath the frilly bedspread. "The mattress comes off in sections," I tell him.

"Why?" he squeaked.

"So you can make someone eat you through the bars."

He replies with a hoarse moan, his lips trembling, the front of his sweatshirt tenting over what has to be a fierce hard-on. I turn around, stunned and more than a little embarrassed by my body's reaction.

Fuck the age gap. It's not like I want to marry him. I just want to see him spread out and begging for it. Surrendered and helpless and all mine. The minute we finish the tour, I'm messaging Karl for clarity, because I might snap if I don't get a piece.

Bullshit. I'm rationalizing. I'm making up reasons to lose control, when I need to be doing the opposite. Though I'll never stop grieving for Pascal—fuck cancer, by the way—I'm happy being single. Happy to get to know myself without a partner to deflect all my shit onto. Not that we weren't good together. We'd been talking about marriage when he got sick. And sure, some people love a hospice wedding, but he was too proud to tie me to him to prove a point.

The last thing I need right now is to start a relationship with a baby gay who's ten years younger and white as all get out, with no job, no house, no plan. He's not just a red flag, he's the whole damn flag factory.

Still, those thighs, and the way they shake as he stumbles around the playroom. It really is a gorgeous space, with exposed brick, a woodstove (complete with branding irons,) and stained glass clerestory windows in the offset roof that paint a rainbow down the opposite wall every afternoon. And yes, it's a strange situation, but I was so broken after losing Pascal that I sold our house a week after the funeral. I couldn't stay there, in those rooms we'd filled with our life together that were now filled with misery, like the smell of sickness and hospital cleaner would never leave the air.

I've done a lot of healing since then. But I'm tempted to stay on here at Niobe and Eric's for a while longer, let that money build. Home ownership is work, and I'm a busy man. Busy living, busy helping my friends pay off their loan, busy getting by, and way too busy to have time for a guy like Reagan.

"So are you like into all this?" he asks, inspecting the row of floggers and flails hanging on the wall near the cross.

"Not as much as some."

"How much?"

"I don't know. Six out of ten."

"Ten being what?"

Karl was right, Reagan does grind your gears. "Why do you want to know?"

"No reason. Just trying to figure some stuff out."

I don't reply. It's none of my business. Karl gave me the run-down on him and Carter's...I don't know, test drive of breaking up, Carter's surprising bout of jealousy getting in the way of a relationship they haven't even started.

Reagan circles the cage bed one last time, his throat moving as he swallows. I'm watching this guy's throat when I should be thinking about making dinner. Or just plain old ignoring him. I'm too old for drama. Looking sadly behind him like a little kid being dragged away from a dinosaur exhibit, he follows me back to the vanilla side of the house, where he disappears into his phone, curled up in a corner of the couch, his knees tucked up under that baggy sweatshirt.

I try not to think about him while I make a fresh pot of genmai-cha, then I head upstairs to put in an unfocused couple of hours editing the next video in my natural calisthenics series. If I don't load it by midnight, a hundred subscribers are going to be up in my inbox by morning, asking if I'm still alive. Chasing those clicks, by which I mean dollars, but I can't catch the flow of my thoughts today, none of the clips matching with what I thought was the theme of the video.

It's not that Reagan's making noise. But I haven't shared my space in so long that I can *feel* him at the edge of my awareness, like the humming of a mosquito while you're trying to fall asleep. I save my shitty draft, upload a few stills to my socials for proof that the video's coming, then give up and go back downstairs.

Reagan's open bag and that big sweatshirt are on the couch, meaning he must be in the bathroom getting dressed. I get some rice going and I'm about to start chopping onions when I hear him.

WYN'S HOUSE

REAGAN

WHY THE FUCK ARE all his friends so hot? Why did Karl think this was a good idea? Why can't I want just one of them? Is what being gay is all about, needing to bang every hot guy that comes within arm's length? Or is it just Carter and his crew who make my dick jump up and my brain shut off?

Which is why I'm locked in Wyn's bathroom, jerking off into the shower stall, because otherwise I'm going to tear off what's left of my clothes and make a complete ass of myself. Not just because he's so hot, with that ripped chest and close cut hair and heavy lidded eyes, but because he's Black, and I'm going to say something wrong.

Look, we're all a product of our upbringing, right? It's not my fault my parents are racist as fuck. And it's easy in this world for a white person with lots of cash to never have to socialize with anyone who isn't also a white person with lots of cash. Until today, I'd never even been in a Black person's house. And yet I'm ready to climb Wyn like a stripper pole, let him fuck the stupid out of me, my blood so hot I can't keep from moaning as the thought of his chestnut hands on my lily white skin sends me over the edge, my come splattering the glossy grey tiles of the shower wall.

Does six out of ten mean he'd make me lick it up? Or is that only a three, and he'd have me tied to the rack with his fist up my ass by now? Why do I want to know?

Question after question, and no one to ask but the internet. Even I'm smart enough to know I won't learn anything that way. I try to use the shower to wash the wall, but it's easier if I just take a shower, which will also give me a reason to have been in here in the first place.

Yet there's nothing I can do about the blush that colours my face as I step out of the tiny bathroom. Wyn is in the kitchen, hunting for something in the little bar fridge, and doesn't notice me or maybe ignores me as I scurry past wrapped in one of his enormous towels.

Karl's packing job is patchy as fuck. He gave me three shirts but no underwear, three individual socks, none of which match, and a pair of track pants that are so dusty they look like he pulled them from under the futon. I have got to find a job so I can stop dressing like trash.

I have to find a job so I can find a place to live then build a fuck room. Somehow I'm supposed to sleep here. I'm supposed to not think about the shit on the other side of that wall. Not think about stepping up onto the blocks at the base of that cross for someone to tie my wrists and ankles to the bolts. Not think about being penned in that little cage, clinging to the bars as I try to reach the flesh that's being held just out of reach...

I glance around but Wyn doesn't seem to have noticed me whimpering. Wearing Karl's sweatshirt (again) with the towel tight around my waist, I step out on the front step to shake the crap off the track pants. The main house on the lot is a big Victorian with some shady renos out back, the newish French doors on the middle floor opening onto thin air, the waterproof paper around them held down by red tape. They've put off fixing their own house to build this sinner's shed, and more power to them. I slip back inside and slip into the sweats, which used to belong to Carter so I have to cinch the drawstring. Swamped by the bigger men's clothes, I look like a bum, like Karl's words came true and I am some homeless kid shuffling from couch to couch.

Take what you've got and be happy, loser. Build some goddamn character. Telling myself this is the only way I'll get through this, the only thing I can tell myself that makes it possible to ignore the gnawing ache in my stomach and the screaming voice in my head that tells me Carter never wants to see me again.

Whatever Wyn is cooking smells amazing, and as I huddle on the couch the warm aromas settle over me like a weighted blanket. He's listening to music as he cooks, some softly pulsing reggae stuff without lyrics and I let myself drift with it, let my eyes droop and my brain turn to mush. His home is small but beautiful, with pale wood flooring and trim and white walls, except for the wall facing the couch, which is painted a leafy green and framed by boxy shelves holding a mix of tropical plants along with little statues of Buddha and Shiva and other characters. One of the plants has sprouted a long vine that he's trained along a couple of hooks at the top of the wall. There's also a few pairs of mounts for resistance bands, and a rack of hand weights on the floor beside one of the bookshelves.

My own fitness routine got torched when I lost access to my condo's gym. I'm going to have to figure something out soon, because if I start getting fat on top of everything else that's going wrong for me, I don't know how I'll cope. And there goes my mood, back to the basement, but before I get going on the internal shit-talking Wyn interrupts by sitting down on the other end of the couch.

"I don't know what you're into but this is pretty much all I eat these days." He offers me one of the deep plates piled high with stir fried greens on top of that multigrain stuff that hipsters ruin sushi with. A good start on my weight control, because unless there's a chicken-fried steak at the bottom of the plate, this meal can't be more than a few hundred calories.

"Smells good," I say as I take the plate. Even though it's probably going to taste like hay. And I have to eat it off my lap like a kid at a grade three birthday party. But this gorgeous guy made it, and the last thing I want to do is insult him. But instead of a squeaky, unchewable mess the kale is soft and sweetly salted, caramelized onions hiding in the folds, and little crispy things that taste so much like bacon that I don't care if they're not.

"Holy shit," I mumble around a mouthful.

"It's good, right?" Grinning, Wyn stabs his fork into another heap of greens, catching one that wasn't cut properly and ends up dangling from his mouth. I nearly spit out my own bite laughing as he tries to work it with his lips. Instead the skinny green flag sticks to his chin. Rolling his eyes, he puts his plate on the floor then goes to the bathroom to wash his face.

"Doesn't anyone on the left own a dining table?" I ask.

Toweling his chin, he shrugs. "I need the space more than I need a table."

"For working out?"

"For making videos. Of working out, before you get all excited."

Am I that fucking obvious? He gets out his phone and pulls up a YouTube channel then hands it to me. His thumbnails aren't much to look at, until I click on one.

"Bro..." He leans over to look and smiles when he sees what I'm watching, a Deep Stretching Routine that's partway between yoga and Pilates and looks like it shouldn't be possible for a person with bones, with a split screen of him doing the same exercise but for beginners. I give him back his phone before my dick gets any harder and my life gets any more complicated. He finishes his plateful while I'm still picking away at the greens, my stomach already settling into siege mode.

"So what exactly is the deal with you and Carter?" Wyn asks as I carry our plates to the kitchen.

"There's no deal. Not with anyone. I think."

"You think?" He raises an eyebrow as my face heats.

"I don't know. I'm out of my comfort zone here. I've never really gotten close to someone before."

"So there's nothing going on but you wish there was?"

"Maybe. I don't know. I don't really know what I'm doing." I look around for a trash can. A compost bucket. Some way to throw out the food on my plate so the sight of it doesn't freak me out any further. I'm yanking open the cupboards blindly when two weights descend on my shoulders. His hands, not gripping me but simply there, warm and solid, his voice soft.

"Breathe, Reagan. It's okay. Just keep breathing."

And I do, because deep down I know it's the only way through. Breathe and let him talk to me, breathe with me, until the ground stops shaking beneath my feet and I can barely remember what pushed me so close to the edge.

"You don't have to tell me anything," he says. "But I'm here if you need me"

I nod and he lets me go. Drained, I wander back to the couch as he starts to tidy the kitchen. I wish I could carry him around in my pocket so I can get him to do that the next time I start to slide. I could have had a very different life.

"I don't know what your plans are for the evening," he says over the sound of running water.

"Plans? I don't have plans anymore."

"I was going to catch up on some shows. You're welcome to watch."

"On what?"

"I have a nice monitor on my desk upstairs."

"In your bedroom?"

"Don't worry, I'll keep my hands to myself."

And I'll keep my thoughts to myself about how much I want those hands on me as I follow him up the death-trap of a tiny staircase that juts out from the wall around the bathroom. The loft is just tall enough for him to walk without stooping, with frosted windows covering one wall and the same Swedish minimalist aesthetic, all pale neutrals and potted plants, strings of little white lights wound through their leaves and wrapped around a birch branch hanging over the desk.

A girl's room, I would have said if you showed me a picture. Yet Wyn doesn't seem out of place, the chill vibe of the space a good match for his energy. Great, I spend one afternoon in a house full of woo and I've already caught hippie brain-rot. It's just a room, just a gigantic bed covered in puffy pillows and a pale green blanket, just a desk with three monitors and a mic, a ring light, and Wyn's spectacular ass, pointing straight at me as he leans over to scroll through the list of episodes. This is a bad, bad, bad idea, being anywhere near a bed with this guy, even if it's just to watch tv. It's a bad idea and I'm totally going to do it.

"Is this alright with you?" he asks as the Doctor Who logo flies out of the electrified mist onscreen.

"Your house. Your rules."

"Don't worry, you don't need to have seen the previous episodes to get what's going on."

Easy for him to say. He's committed to it, hissing and cheering, sometimes gasping in shock, his fist pressed to his lips. I can't find the thread of the plot, which involves a bunch of British people running around waving things that aren't guns at people who may or may not have been the bad guys.

After a couple of episodes my eyes are itching, and I lay my head back on the pillows. I wake up with a start, my face wedged against something warm and solid: Wyn's shoulder.

"Shit, sorry," I mumble as I struggle upright.

"It's alright. You look wrecked."

"I guess. I haven't been sleeping well." Not just recently but ever, no matter how much I want it, my mind always leaping ahead, finding new things to panic about, unless I drug it into silence. "Aren't you going to try to sell me a miracle cure?"

He chuckles in his chest. "Not every fitness influencer is a shady motherfucker. Some of us are just trying to get by."

"I was kidding."

"I know."

I rub my aching eyes, wondering if he has proper painkillers or just herbs in a gelatin cap. The day started so well and is ending so weirdly, sitting in this stranger's bed, insulting him without even trying. Burning another bridge before I've had a chance to cross it.

"You okay?" he asks, briefly touching my knee.

I start nodding but my body knows the truth and it turns into shaking my head. I am not, have not been, have never been okay, and everything I've done in my life has been done to keep this a secret.

"I'm here if you want to talk," he murmurs.

"You people sure love to talk," I spit, bitter with tension. "Don't you ever just do a thing? Act without calculating all the social costs?"

"I used to," he says, folding his hands in his lap. "Those were some hard lessons to learn."

"So now you're above it all?"

"Did I say that?"

He gazes at me not with anger but with a cool neutrality that reminds me who has all the power, and that it's not me. I may be his guest, but I'm everyone's guest, dependent on other people's kindness to survive. My next words will make or break me, but is there any way to play this that won't end in disaster? Not when every choice I make leads to a new kind of catastrophe. But if every road before me ends in a cliff or a brick wall, what difference does it make which one I choose?

Wyn's expression softens. "What is it, Reagan?"

"Will you let me suck your dick?"

He twists to look and me head on, his mouth falling open. "The fuck?"

"I'm really good at it. I think. And I have, like, zero gag reflex."

"What the hell? Why did you even offer?"

"I don't know." And I don't, can't remember why I thought it was a good idea. Why I thought he'd want me. Disaster after disaster, and I grind my fists into my eyes, willing away my humiliating tears. So many tears, like I lost my manhood when I lost that job. Like everything I believed about myself was a lie.

But when I go to get up off the bed he grabs my wrist. A firm yet gentle grip, his hand encircling my narrow wrist. "But I thought—"

"I'm not gonna fuck you," he says with a chuckle. "Just lie here with me."

"But—"

"Lie the fuck down, brat."

I do, because he wants me to, and he pulls me into his arms. Solidly sculpted arms that cage me against his broadly muscled chest, and now every single part of me is stiff as steel as I lie in his embrace.

"You are one touch starved little man," he murmurs, settling his chin on the top of my head. "Your parents weren't huggers, were they?"

A bitter laugh escapes my frozen mouth. Then a sob. Then another, and with my arms pinned to my chest I can't hold them in, can't hold back the tidal wave of tears.

"Why do I keep losing my shit?" I sniffle into his shirt when the worst has passed.

"Maybe you have a lot of shit to get rid of."

"Is that why it feels like I'm going to puke?" I groan, my stomach knotting around my meal.

He huffs a laugh, his breath ruffling my hair. "You puke in my bed and you're buying me a new mattress."

"Maybe I should go downstairs."

"Or maybe just relax? I'll put on a progressive relaxation exercise."

Back to that HR session, only this meditation is narrated by a Black woman's beautiful voice and not that drawling chick from Kelowna. Instead of a yoga mat on a board room floor, I'm lying in a pillowy bed under fairy lights, listening to Wyn's steady breathing beside me as the disembodied voice drifting from the speakers hidden in the headboard leads me through tensing and relaxing every part of my body in turn. I don't remember if we ever got to the head and shoulders. Maybe I fell asleep.

APOLOGIES

CARTER

IF I DIDN'T ALREADY live with Karl, I'd spend all damn day on chat with him, offloading my bullshit and begging for his advice, because once again he was right. He knew Trey was going to cheat, he knew five years ago that my parents were going to split up, and he knew that deep down I'm full of the fear that I can't ever trust my partners.

Reagan isn't even mine, just a guy that I'm helping, a young man I'm trying to keep off the streets. Like I'm the fucking Salvation Army. I lean into my groan as I press the last reps with the chest bar. Karl, and working out: as good as any therapist I've had for helping me see past the end of my nose, see where my actions have contributed to the fucked up situation I'm facing.

The truth is, I acted irrationally. I let a momentary emotion overcome my better judgement, let my ego drive the bus right off a cliff. What did Reagan even do? Buy some new clothes, sing into a mop handle, make a cringe video. When I was in my twenties I had bangs and a MySpace page with rotating axes in the header (because I was so metal, right?)

And in the end, it's none of my business what he does with his life. Who he dates, who he fucks, none of it. He's just a friend that I'm helping.

He is not mine.

The truth of this is so heavy I almost can't finish the last rep, but I'm not going to yell for a spot just because I'm pining for a libertarian snowflake with pretty eyes. I'm not pining. I'm...

I don't know. I sit on the bench for a few minutes catching my breath and trying to figure out exactly what to call this sickening lump in my stomach. I can't stop seeing the fear, the hurt in those pretty eyes as I kicked him out of the only home he has.

Remorse: that lump in my stomach is remorse. We're not on equal ground, Reagan and I. I have all the power, and all he has is my tolerance. At least Karl found him before he got too far and set him up at Wyn's. At least I have friends who are smarter than me.

Whatever happens, I have to accept that I have no claim on Reagan.

He is not, can never be mine.

I'll survive. He's one man among millions. There's enough we don't agree on that there's no hope of us staying together. People don't change overnight, and I'm not looking for a project. I want someone with goals. Realistic goals like moving out of Toronto so we can afford to buy a house, or maybe getting a dog. Not making bank on a crypto swindle then blowing it all on bottle service and hair gel.

Except I don't know that he'd still make that choice. Something in him has changed, some tension he was holding onto easing as he comes out his shell. He doesn't jump at every noise the way he did the first week. Or gel his hair every day, or complain about taking the streetcar or Karl's yodeling in the shower, which even I have a hard time tolerating. Reagan has changed, and so have I, and it wasn't for the better.

The bright morning has passed, and I trudge home from the gym through a steady drizzling mist that flattens my hair to my head and matches my self-loathing. I've never thought of myself as jealous. I've sure never fought anyone over a crush. Even when Trey admitted to sleeping with Gregor, I wasn't jealous of the hookup so much as angry that Trey lied to me. Karl is reading in the living room when I get home, but I ignore him until I change clothes and don't feel so soggy. He hasn't moved, curled up on the couch with a little blanket over his legs even though it's the middle of summer. He senses me in the doorway and closes his book, keeping his place with his finger.

"I'm sorry for what I said before," I mumble, feeling half my age. "I accused you of something awful for no reason. And Reagan too. It was just a video."

"He sent it to me also," Karl replies levelly, but his words knock me sideways.

"Why the fuck did you tell me that?" I groan.

"Why should I hide it from you? It shows that he meant nothing by it."

"Yeah but...ah shit." I deflate, slumping against the doorframe. "You're right. He probably has no idea how I read him."

"Now he does."

"Because I called him a bunch of names then threw him out of my house. What the hell is my problem?"

"I have my theories, but—"

"Get bent."

"I think already did that, yes? Isn't that a British word for gay as hell?"

Smart and a smart ass, but Karl's a solid friend and has forgiven me for plenty, though maybe nothing this avoidable. He puts his book aside and gets up to hug me.

"Now, call your boy and apologize to him also," he says as he returns to his spot on the couch.

"He's not my boy," I grumble as I get out my phone.

"Yet," Karl murmurs, disappearing behind his book.

"Stop saying that. There's nothing going on."

"Yet."

"Say 'yet' again, motherfucker,"

He giggles, wriggling into the couch. "You are stressing for no reason. He's not gone forever. You can still win him."

"I don't want to *win him*, thank you, Jane Austen."

"Perhaps he yearns for you as you yearn for him."

"Just stop. All I want to do is apologize."

"And then?"

"And then what? We go back to how it was."

Karl says nothing more, making one of what Wyn and I call his Balkan faces, pouting and rolling his eyes like my Romanian grandmother used to, but I'm not taking the bait. This isn't the first time living with Karl has felt like being married to him.

Because he knows me too well. Knows that I want Reagan, that maybe I really do yearn for him. It's ridiculous, and doomed, and I can't stop thinking what if. What if we tried to get past our differences? What if I really do live in an echo chamber, othering a huge section of the population just because they did it to me first? Since moving in, Reagan has done his best to fit in. To be helpful. To listen more than he speaks, which surprised me then became normalized. He's trying so hard to grow, and all I saw was the surface.

It takes me until almost midnight to be happy with my text. It's only a few words inviting him over tomorrow. *No bad news* I add at the last second. Once it's sent, I feel deflated, like I gave away a secret, and I take a dropper of CBD oil then put myself to bed. Before Papa Karl scolds me again.

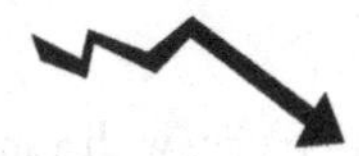

Reagan replies early the next morning with his usual couple of letters in lieu of actual words. He comes by a few hours later, leaving his things at Wyn's. Standing on our doormat in his borrowed clothes—a pair of my sweatpants and a t-shirt branded with Wyn's YouTube channel—he looks both proud and pitiful, his hands clenched to fists, dark shadows around his eyes as he waits for me to speak.

Time to do some adulting, Carter. "There's no easy way to say this, so I'll just go for it and tell you that I'm sorry. I accused you without proof, and really it's none of my business who you get involved with. I offered you a room because you needed the help, not because I want anything in return. So if you want to come back, that's fine. In fact, I'd like it if you did."

"Are you sure?"

"Totally. Wyn doesn't have room for you anyway."

"Yeah, I ended up crashing in his bed. We didn't do anything," he adds quickly as I suck in a breath. "We were watching Doctor Who and I fell asleep."

"You like Doctor Who?"

"Wyn wanted to watch. I was just there for someone to hang out with. But he got me thinking, with his videos and stuff. I can't keep mooching off you guys. If I'm going to keep living here. I should be contributing to the household budget, right?" The two of us flinch as Karl pops out of the kitchen.

"Are you going to start an OnlyFans?" he asks, grinning behind his beard. Trust him to go for the jugular. "It's a job like any other," he says as I groan and Reagan's face goes white. "If you're willing to pay to watch porn, shouldn't you be willing to get paid for making some?"

"But isn't that like prostitution?" Reagan says, half whispering the word.

"So what if it was?" Karl replies with a shrug.

"But people don't...I guess some people do."

"A lot more than you think. Especially those who aren't given a lot of other chances. But don't you start tricking," he says, wagging his finger like a sit-com mom. "A rabbit like you would get himself murdered by the end of the first week."

"Excuse me, rabbit?" Reagan chokes.

"Why not?" Karl says, his smile spreading. "You're small, cute, and edible."

"Who the fuck eats rabbits?"

Karl growls, clawing the air. "I do, Flopsy." Cackling, he goes back in the kitchen as Reagan turns to me with a little boy's pout.

"Can I at least be Bugs Bunny?" he asks.

"How about I meet you halfway, Thumper?"

"Who the fuck is Thumper?" he says, frowning.

"You've never seen *Bambi*?"

"I haven't seen shit. My parents didn't let me watch movies."

"What did you do for fun?"

"I didn't really have time for fun," he says with a one-sided shrug.

"Is that why you're so uptight?"

"Way to go, doc, another successful diagnosis," he replies bitterly. Then he sighs, rubbing his forehead. "Sorry. Yes, obviously that's what turned me into an anxious overachiever with daddy issues. Shit. Can you fuck me or something?"

"No."

"What? Why not?"

"I think you need to sit with the discomfort"

He sags on his feet, making a face. "Ugh, why?" he groans. "Do you want me to be miserable?"

"Not exactly, but maybe you need to *let* yourself be miserable. Stop numbing yourself with sex and drugs and toxic behavior. If you're miserable, be miserable. Don't fight your feelings. That's how they get stuck and end up messing you up later."

He sighs again. "Okay, but will you fuck me later? Shit, forget I even said that," he groans, rubbing his eyes. "I'm such a loser."

"You're not. I don't hang out with losers. Straight to block. If I didn't believe that you're a decent person behind all your weird bullshit, I wouldn't have done any of this for you. I would have handed back your wallet, said have a nice day, then walked away. Might have tried to tap your ATM card at the grocery store first."

"Shit. That's probably what I would have done. If I even bothered to look for you. Goddamn it, I'm such a... No. I *used* to be such a fuck up. I'm going to get this right, I promise."

Poised on the threshold—of my house and my life—Reagan is trembling with emotion, his eyes wide and pleading. This moment means something to him, so I better not screw it up. Give in to my first and worst instinct to pull him into my arms and kiss away his fears. Too soon, when I still don't know how much of me I want to give.

"It's okay, Reagan," I say, griping his shoulder, giving myself that much. "You'll be okay."

He nods, biting his lip, fighting an unspeakable battle against something bigger than me, bigger than him. Whatever it is that turned him into this brittle, self-hating shill for his own exploitation. All those parts of his past that taught him that real men don't cry, that love is a joke, that faith is for gamblers and hate always wins.

But it doesn't. Not today, as put my arms around him and hold him as he shatters. Sobbing out the pain of years, of his whole life, until I'm crying too, because maybe he's human after all.

HELL BENT

KARL

ONE OF THE BEST innovations to appear in my lifetime is noise-cancelling headphones. I do not want to accidentally listen to Carter and Reagan kiss and make up. Their making up is bad enough, because despite all I've said about being a good person, I wouldn't have been sad if they had split for good. If Reagan had moved out, so that I might call him in a few months and shoot my shot, as the kids say, without seeming like I'm outflanking my friend.

Lost in my book, I don't notice time passing until I feel the old house vibrate as someone closes the front door. Hounded by the mental Greek chorus of my mother's insistence to *at least make an attempt, Karolla*, I put aside my book, abandon my cone of silence, and leave my room.

"Hey!" Dropping his bag, Reagan bounds towards me. He skids to a halt, grinning, panting, messily adorable with his unshaven chin and handed down clothes, his fair cheeks as pink as his lips. Lips I need to stop staring at if I want to carry my end of the conversation.

"So. You kissed and made up?" I say to him.

He jerks back. "What do you mean, kissed?" he asks, looking around as if for witnesses.

"My mistake," I reply softly as hope leaps up in my chest.

"Me and Carter, we're just friends."

"Of course."

"And hey, that was stupid of me, to send you those videos," he says with a grimace.

"Forget them. I've seen worse on TikTok. Just today in fact, here, I'll show you."

He laughs as I reach for my phone. "I believe you. Hell, you weren't wrong about OnlyFans. I should make a few more vids, get monetized."

My turn to laugh. "You should think about getting a job. Not one of your fancy baller finance contracts but work like ordinary people do. Retail. Office admin. Money in your pocket."

"So I can give some of it to you?"

"Electricity doesn't grow on trees."

"I know, I know. I'll figure something out."

"Hey, as long as you're trying."

"Yes, Dad," he says in a kid's tired sing-song, fluttering his lashes. "But tonight I'm not doing shit. We're ordering a pizza and I'm drinking some beer and going the fuck to sleep. Wyn's great but the rabbit food, man..." He shakes his head in wonderment. "How is he so ripped without eating meat?"

"Genetics. And far more devotion than I will ever have." I gesture to my tummy, which isn't the biggest it's been but is still the first thing about me most people see.

"Aw, but I like your papa belly," Reagan says, poking me in the middle of it. "You're like Jack Black hot, but before he got all pissy about that shooter."

"Where did you learn about that?" I ask as he prances towards the front door. He turns with a look of innocence.

"Um, a little thing called the internet? Come on, Karl, do some research."

By the end of the week, I have lost all faith in myself. He consumes my thoughts. He's always there. He's no one's, but he can't be mine because I can't betray my friend. My friend who watches him whenever he is in the room. Who sulks whenever Reagan leaves the apartment and brightens when he returns. Who must want him as much as I do, though I can't make myself ask. Better to dream in blissful ignorance than have my worst fears confirmed.

Over the years I have watched Carter fall in and out of love. He had so much invested in Trey, though if he'd asked me I'd have told him to give up months ago. I can't blame him for not going after Reagan this soon after having his heart bruised, if not outright broken. And so we watch, and want, and wonder—or at least I do—how long until one of us surrenders.

Luckily my work keeps me at the bookstore late more than once, preparing for a major author's signing on the weekend. Finding me asleep in one of the chairs in the reading nook on Friday afternoon, my boss lets me clock out early. The 501 streetcar is under construction again, so I start home on foot, letting the mellow sunshine and the buzz of human life swirling around me wear away my rough edges. Every face is a new sort of face, from every nation on earth, drawn to Canada by the promise of stability, of continuity, of a life free from horror and fear. Not all discover it, like the unhoused woman I pass sheltering behind a shopping cart at the foot of Nathan Phillips Square.

But still. I rarely speak of my life before emigration. Most people are not ready for that scale of devastation. It builds a wall between us, a bourgeois discomfort with admitting how evil humans can be to each other. It is a privilege not to know.

But still.

I am alive, I am free. I am employed in a job I truly love, even when it challenges me. I have friends, and I love them as well. I have choice. And so I keep walking, soaking up the sun, smiling when I catch someone's eye, making my own happiness. When I reach McCaul I turn right by habit. But why shouldn't I stop at one of my favorite shops, treat myself to the sort of book my store won't stock? A poetry chapbook, or a little erotica. Probably the latter, as I have always preferred to read about sex rather than watch it performed.

Hell Bent for Leather sells far more than books, which are rather in the minority. The rest of the co-op's storefront is filled with merchandise more to Baldwin's taste, him and his landlords and the other kinky folk. If it can be inserted into, buckled around, or slapped against someone's naughty parts, you'll find it here, and I tour around the shop, marveling at the opportunities. And the prices. As I flip through the book rack, Misty and Sabine, two of the principle members of the co-op's board, come out from the back carrying boxes.

"All I'm saying is, he'd better get his shit together," Sabine says. She sets down her box and begins to load bottles of lube onto the shelf. "I don't care that Mary wants to do that to him. I'm not her."

"I know, Little," Misty says tiredly, massaging her temples with her fingertips. "I don't like it any more than you do."

"Damn straight I don't like it. I—oh. Sorry, Karl." Her face darkens as she goes back to stocking the shelf, setting down the bottles with force as I approach the counter with a miraculously clean secondhand copy of *While Standing in Line Waiting for Death*.

"Trouble in paradise? I murmur as Misty rings it up.

"More like too many cooks in the kitchen," she replies, rolling her heavy eyes.

"May I ask you something?" I say as I slip the book into my shoulder bag. "A personal question?"

"Shoot."

"How does someone know if they are polyamorous?" Misty rolls her eyes again as Sabine snorts a laugh.

"Honestly, I think everyone is a little bit," Misty says, leaning her bosom on the counter like a buxom bartender about to save my soul. "I think monogamy's the outlier. If you look at human evolution, human nature."

"We're all just waiting for our metamour to ride up on a white stallion?"

"I'm not saying it's easy," Misty goes on as Sabine starts to properly cackle. "My point is, polyam is what you make it. Sometimes it's a cuddle puddle and co-housing, but sometimes it's like a constellation and there's no cross-over between metamours. Not everyone has to be equally attached to each other. Your partner's lover doesn't become your lover by default."

"That would be a bold presumption."

"Especially if the center is bi. If you were seeing a straight woman and a gay man, you wouldn't expect them to fuck each other."

"Good luck with finding a gay man who'd date a bisexual."

"Tell me about it," Misty says wryly.

"I don't get what that's all about," Sabine says, squeezing past Misty with the empty box. "Do they think they're going to catch straight from the leftover cooch on your—"

"Sab, customers," Misty mutters to her as the door opens, setting off the bell which they've replaced with a sample of a whip cracking.

"So what's this about, anyway?" Sabine asks me as Misty goes to greet the blow-dried white suburbanite blinking at the rack of floggers. "Are you and Carter thinking about opening your relationship?"

"I'm sorry? What relationship?"

Her lip curling, she looks me up and down. "Dude, you guys have been living together for like two years."

"Yes. We're roommates."

"Sure you are."

"We are. I swear!"

"Dude, I don't care."

"Well, I do. Is that why I can't hook up in this city? Because everyone thinks I'm taken? Did you also think this?" I ask Misty as she rejoins us.

"It's sort of a known thing," she says with a guilty shrug.

"Plus you're bisexual," Sabine chirps.

"Thanks for announcing it to the room."

"Hey, now. No bi erasure," she replies with a stern little frown. "Even self-erasure."

"That doesn't mean I need it broadcast. Why don't you take out a billboard: Karl Veselko fucks anyone who wants it."

"You'd probably hook up more often, just saying."

"I don't want to hook up. I want to meet someone worth my time. Someone who cares about more than his abs and who said what to Chappell Roan."

"Hey. Don't you be coming for Chappell," Sabine says sharply. "And isn't this the sort of thing you should be telling your therapist?"

"I do tell him. He says I need to get out there more."

"He's got a point," Misty muses. "You're not going to meet anyone by sitting around at home."

She's right and she's wrong. I did meet someone by staying home. Someone I can't have. Thankfully he's not there when I get back, for his shoes aren't by the door. Wyn's gleaming white sneakers are, however, and for a moment I consider slipping out again before I have to engage in conversation.

"Reagan?" Carter calls from the sitting room.

Too late. "No, it's me."

"Good timing," he says, coming to the doorway. "Me and Wyn are planning for the cottage."

"What do you think," Baldwin asks I as come into the room. "Should we invite Reagan?"

"Do we have to?"

They exchange looks. "No, but I think he'd enjoy it," Wyn replies. "Plus Mr. Chambers here is bugging about leaving him on his own."

"I'm not bugging," Carter retorts. "I just don't know if I totally trust him to spend a week alone and not do something dumb."

"The parents are out of town, let's throw a party?" I say.

"No. Well, maybe. Can you imagine what his friends are like?"

"He says he doesn't have any," Wyn offers.

"Not until he tells them he's got somewhere they can come with their women and drugs." I mutter.

"He's not a child," Carter says to me sharply.

"Do you not want him at the cottage?" Wyn asks me.

"In so many words. It's our *thing*. It's settled, it's comfortable. I like the quiet, I like the space. He's not our pet, we don't have to bring him with us everywhere."

"Personally, I don't mind if he comes," Wyn says, looking between us. "Kid needs some nature therapy."

"You obviously want him to come so you can fuck him," I say to Carter, who groans, dropping his head in his hands.

"That's not why."

"No? That's only a bonus feature?"

He sits up to glare at me. "For fuck's sake, Karl, stop imagining I'm boning him. No, stop projecting your own horny bullshit onto me."

Damn. Caught. Because of course he is right, this is my fear speaking. My fear of being left behind, but I can't keep going like this, second guessing my friend, living on a precipice.

"You can't tell me that you *don't* want him," I say.

Wyn lets out a low whistle. "What?" he says as we both glare at him. "I didn't do a thing. I didn't ask him to suck my dick, he asked me."

"He did what?" I bark as Carter jumps to his feet.

"You mean he didn't tell you?" Wyn says. "Shit, what's that boy's game?"

"I don't have a game."

We fall silent, turning to Reagan standing in the doorway. He's been running, his face flushed and sweaty, his shirt glued to his chest.

"Seriously, I'm not trying to play you guys," he says, taking a few steps into the room. "You're friends. I don't want to come between you. So if you need me to move out—"

"That's not the problem," Carter blurts. "There is no problem. Right?" Wyn and I nod, because there shouldn't be a problem. Reagan is not the problem. We are.

"Alright, cool," he replies, nodding slowly at each of us. "I'm going to grab a shower, in that case."

He ducks out of the room, and I bite my lip to stop from calling him back. Calling him to us to see if he'll come. This pet I pretend I don't want.

"I'll go ask him about the cottage," Carter says, staring after him. He leaves the room without waiting for our reply.

"You okay, Karl?" Wyn asks as I drop into the nearest chair.

"I can't help feeling left out. I'm the only one of us who's dick he hasn't tried to suck."

TAGALONG

REAGAN

What just happened? What did I just walk into? Because they were talking about me. I went to prep school, I know when a group of people have been talking behind my back: the flinch, the guilty flick of their eyes, the quick agreement with whatever the alpha dog said. Carter, in this case, because he's the one who found me. Picked me up off the side of the road like a stray. Tried to leave me behind, but I followed him home.

Do I want to be kept? There's something intoxicating about this dependence. I've done nothing but work, for as long as I can remember. Chasing bank because in some twisted way I thought money could insulate me from everyone and everything I feared. That the more I earned, the more I was worth, on some abstract scale of human value that had nothing to do with how good a person I was. All of that erased in a couple of keystrokes, yet here I was, still the same man, still alive, still striving.

I stick my head under the shower spray, blurring out the world, wishing the water could wash away my wasted years. A smart man would have saved against this moment. Taken dividends and stashed them in a tax-free account. Built a future instead of letting the bet ride. Hard lessons that I should have learned in business school, not at the wrong end of a crime that no one can be bothered to prosecute.

Yet I never saw myself as greedy until now, thinking about all three of those men being in charge of me. I slap at the hot tap, cutting the flow so the water runs cold, shocking me out of my daydream. I'm reading too much into that moment, those few words. Making assumptions is why Carter threw me out. I won't make the same mistake, not even if it's what I want.

Enough. I need get to out of the shower and get dressed before I start feeling myself up. I hang my sweaty running clothes over the shower rail so they don't rot in the laundry hamper (yes, Papa Karl) then hustle to my room. When I come out, Carter is standing in his doorway.

"Can we talk?"

"Sure." I expect him to step into the hall but he retreats into his room. Great, a private talk in Carter's bedroom, right when I've decided not to make assumptions.

Not like that stops me.

I've never been in here. He needs to start letting me in so I can clean, because the college dorm vibe is brutal. I ignore the piles of books and paper on his dresser and dirty laundry on his floor and concentrate on Carter who's chewing his upper lip the way he does when out of his comfort zone.

"Wyn says you tried to rec center him," he says, his voice rough but low.

"What? Oh. Yeah. I did. He said no."

"So he said."

"Are you mad?"

"I was, at first. But it's none of my business. You're still figuring yourself out. I can't stand in the way."

"You're not in the way. It was a dumb thing to do."

"You're just young. And you're kind of not great with people after being raised by narcissistic assholes in a hyper competitive milieu where every relationship was transactional."

Trust Carter to pack a whole sociology lesson into a single sentence. "I'm with you on the narcissistic assholes, and I'm going to assume the rest means more of the same, so yeah. I'm that."

"That's okay. You're learning."

"Am I ever," I say, tugging at Karl's sweatshirt, which might as well be mine at this point. "A couple months ago I was in the back of a stretch Hummer, snorting ketamine off a media executive's girlfriend's wrist."

"Damn. And now you're couch surfing in Parkdale."

"It is what it is. I'm not knocked out though. Just winded."

"You'll get back on your feet. And don't worry about moving out. We're all grown-ups here, we'll make it work, even if there's a little friction."

"Are you sure?"

"Positive. In fact, we wanted to invite you to come camping with us."

"Camping?"

"Cottaging, really," he says with a guilty smirk. "We used to camp. But Karl's got back problems and I hate sleeping on the ground, so we upgraded a few years ago."

"I wouldn't be in the way?"

"There's four bedrooms. They're small, but you wouldn't be sleeping on the couch or anything. "

Not exactly what I meant, but I let it slide. Whatever he's offering, I'm taking. He explains the details though I don't pay much attention. I'm more interested in the fact that they're including me in what sounds like a long-standing tradition.

"As long as it won't be weird, having me there."

"We'd like you to be there."

"I don't really have cottage clothes."

"We'll hit the second hand shop, score you some Timberlands and a flannel jacket."

"How about we don't do that?"

"Don't stress, Reagan," he says, clapping me on the arm. "The cottage is the opposite of stress. Just the trees and the sky and the water."

"There is a cottage right?"

"Yes. There's a cottage."

The cottage is both better and worse than I expect. I mean, the sexual tension during the three and a half hour drive north in a rented 4x4 is off the fucking charts, but no one's talking about that.

If you're not Canadian that may seem like a long way to go to relax, but the cottage is an icon of bourgeois achievement, a summer ritual for tens of thousands of city residents who load their cars with boxed snacks and bug spray then drive three hundred kilometers to sit and look at a lake. My idea of a vacation destination usually involves all-you-can-drink fees and getting hit on by sunburnt South African millionaires. Maybe sitting on my ass looking at a lake isn't such a bad idea.

I keep thinking we've arrived, as every turn puts us onto a smaller and bumpier road, until we're creeping along an overgrown tunnel of trees. Beside me in the back, Karl is staring straight ahead like he's expecting something to appear out of the green. No one has said much for the last half hour, and I yelp when Wyn stops the car suddenly.

"Sorry, but it's giving major psycho killer at summer camp," I say as Carter gets out to drag the fallen sapling off the so-called road.

"It's private property," Karl answers. "An old friend of Wyn's homeowners."

"Used to be a nudist colony," Wyn says over his shoulder. "Private lake and all."

"Sun's out, buns out?"

"If you feel like getting your white ass burnt."

"Imagine how much it must hurt to get a sunburn on your willy," Karl muses as Carter gets back into the truck.

"The fuck?" He twists to glare at Karl. "Do I even want to know what you're all talking about?"

"Sunburns," Karl replies, beaming.

Shaking his head, Carter settles back in his seat as Wyn puts the truck in gear. A few minutes later we come out of the woods and into a cleanly swept patch of sandy soil surrounded by mixed stands of trees. Gathering as much as I can carry, I follow the guys along a mulched path between the trees to a low cabin sided with rough-edged boards. It looks too small for all of us, but I keep my thoughts to myself until we get inside.

"Woah..."

"It's had a few additions," Carter says, grinning as I stare around me. The property slopes towards the water and the cottage is a back-split, with a wall of soaring windows that look out across the lake. A great layout, if only the place wasn't a museum, every piece of furniture and décor lifted straight from fifty years ago.

"It's like the set of Stranger Things," I murmur. "Doesn't your friend want to update it?"

"It's the cottage," Carter replies with a frown. "Don't mess with success."

"Yeah, but dude..." I point to the orange and gold abstract wall hanging that looks like furry cheese, the ceramic chickens on the kitchen counters.

"What? It's like my grandma's cottage on Lake Erie."

"Cleaner water though," Wyn says, nodding to the lake.

"Definitely. Can you believe I used to swim at her place?"

"Did I hear someone say swimming?" Karl says. Water shoes slapping off the linoleum, he emerges from a side room, dressed to go: sunblock on his nose, a towel around his waist.

"No, Karl, just you," Wyn says with a laugh.

"Dude, we haven't even unpacked the car," Carter groans.

"I'll help." Karl unwraps his towel and hangs it over the rail of the landing, revealing a pair of tiny navy blue swim shorts.

"Shit, Karl," I blurt. "Are you a shower or a grower?"

"Beg your pardon?"

"Never mind." I don't want to make him self-conscious, because then he might change clothes and rob me of the sight of his cock struggling to be contained by the bare minimum.

When we've ferried everything inside, Carter shows me to my room. It's even narrower than my bedroom at home (his home, that is) and full of more old décor, a trio of ducks in flight made of hammered copper hanging on the wall, a crocheted cover on the tissue box on the wobbly side table.

"What's so funny" he asks as I snicker to myself.

"My boss—my old boss—Ajay wanted to buy a place in Muskoka. Basically a condo on the lake. He'd have bulldozed this without a thought. Don't get me wrong, I kind of like it now that I'm used to it. But that's funny in itself, how few fucks I'm starting to give about money and prestige and everything. Here I am at this place my boss would tear down, wearing other men's old clothes, trying to decide if I'm polyam—"

Shit. He's not supposed to know. Not yet, while I'm still figuring myself out, like he said the other day.

"No, I don't want to talk about it," I blurt as he takes a breath. He exhales with a wry smile.

"Fair enough. You know where I am if you do."

As he leaves the room I drop onto the creaky old bed and cover my face with the musty pillow. It doesn't matter what I do, I'm still playing them against each other. Waiting for one of them to make up his mind, so I don't have to.

BACKTO BASICS

WYN

My bomb nearly blew up the cottage trip, but I don't let shit like that get in the way of my friendships, or of this tradition. Some of us are even more devoted, like Karl, who needs to get in the lake as soon as possible after arrival. Carter goes down to the shore with him while I watch from the comfortable distance of the deck.

The screen door slides open and Reagan comes outside, a pillow crease printed across his cheek. Stopping by my chair, he yawns, stretching his arms over head and showing his stomach. I go back to watching Karl, who's hooting as he dunks himself in the chilly water. It doesn't matter what I think of Reagan's stomach, how much I want to run my tongue round his pert little belly button and down to his...

It doesn't matter. Carter met him first. But when Reagan gets his feet under him and isn't living in their house, the calculations change. Even though I never thought I'd feel anything like this again, this pull of attraction, this curiosity about another person.

He leans on the rail, pointing his ass at me. Not on purpose, I remind myself as he stretches, arching his back.

"Is it always this quiet?" he asks.

"Yep. Sometimes you can hear big motors on the bay, or a plane. That's about it."

"Wild. I don't know if I could take it, all year round."

"Me neither. I hate shoveling snow."

"I meant more that I'd be bored out of my mind."

"You definitely gotta enjoy your own company."

"Then I'd definitely snap."

"Don't like yourself much?"

He sighs, gazing across the lake as the wind tugs at his loose hair. He's changed since that night he spent at my place, his hard edges softened. "Does it matter if I like myself?" he asks, not looking my way. "I'd settle for not hating myself."

"Take it one day at a time."

"Is that some kind of mantra?"

"No. It's the only choice you have. You can't make the future you want happen by thinking about it. You have to act in the now to get you to that future."

"Act in the now," he muses. "Otherwise the future stays in the future."

"You got it."

Karl has clambered out of the water and stands streaming wet on the pebbly shore. "Aren't you coming for a swim?" he shouts, his hands cupped around his mouth. "It's lovely."

"It looks cold," Reagan calls to him.

"Nonsense. You can't tell from looking."

"Does he really think I'm going in that water?" he asks me.

"Why not? I do. Just not first thing on arrival. But get a little indica in me tomorrow afternoon and we'll get out the inflatables."

Karl and Carter join us on the deck, Karl still dripping beneath the towel over his shoulders, his skin bright pink from the water, which even in the middle of summer is usually colder than I like.

"It's no problem if you don't have a bathing suit," Karl says to Reagan. "Nudist colony, remember?"

"Not having a suit isn't what worries me. It's more that my nuts are going to suck up into my chest cavity."

"Oh, that will happen anyway," Karl replies, grinning. "I think mine are somewhere around here." He holds his hand flat near his throat.

"Which is why I'm still dry."

"We can change that," Karl says tossing the towel off his shoulders like a cape as he stalks towards Reagan. "Come here, boy, and let me sit on your lap."

He lunges at Reagan who leaps away from him, squealing. As he dashes back inside the house, leaving the screen open for Karl to follow him, Carter lowers himself into the chair beside mine.

"Was this a bad idea?" he asks.

"Time will tell."

"I didn't want him to be lonely. I don't know why it matters, though. He's not really my friend."

"Are you sure?"

He glances towards the cottage. "Alright, so we're friends. But I don't want to fuck up our circle for someone I've only known a few months."

"I'm good. If you and him want to go for it—"

"I didn't say that."

"But if you did, it's cool with me."

"You're the one who called him a snack."

"Because he's a hot piece of ass."

"But would you?"

"Why do you want to know so badly?"

Before Carter answers, Karl and Reagan come back outside, Karl with his damn plum brandy and four shot glasses.

"Come, Baldwin, is it really the cottage if we do not toast?" he says as I make a face.

"Okay, but put it away after. Shit's like candy, I'll want to drink the whole bottle."

"You say that like it's a bad thing," he replies, grinning wickedly.

"It *is* a bad thing, getting wrecked. I want to enjoy myself."

Karl hands round the little glasses full of pinkish brown liquor. A recipe he got from his Croatian grandma, the stuff tastes like honey and hits like jet fuel.

"Here's to old friends and new," Karl says, raising his glass.

"Here's to trying new things," Reagan says, grinning at him.

"Here's to getting back to basics," I say, because that's what I like best about coming here, the freedom from the stifling, striving modern world.

"I don't know," Carter says with a sigh. "I guess, here's to it not raining all week."

"Shit. You know you can't say that out loud," I say as Karl groans. "Now it's gonna rain for sure."

"It's not," Carter says, gesturing at the pristine blue above us. "Look at that sky."

"Whatever, if we're stuck inside tomorrow I'm blaming you."

"Gentlemen," Karl says firmly. "Our toast, if you will." We drink, the sugary sweetness of the plums masking the kick of the strong liquor. Smacking his lips, Karl sets down his glass with a clunk.

"If it's going to rain, then I'm going swimming while I still can. You're sure you won't join me?" he says to Reagan, who recoils.

"No way. That water's freezing."

"It's been colder."

"I'll come down with you," Carter says, hauling himself out of the deep Adirondack chair. As they thud down the wooden stairs to the lawn, Reagan wanders to the front of the deck again.

"So what's up with Karl?" he asks, leaning his elbows on the railing.

"What do you mean?"

"He's like a different person. He's really quiet at home."

"So am I."

He frowns at me over his shoulder. "You're literally just sitting there."

"Give me time to recover from the drive." Karl whistles and Reagan sighs.

"Okay, but I'm not going in past my knees," he shouts in reply. "He's not going to throw me in the deep part, is he?" he asks me.

"Not if you don't want him to."

He stares at me for a beat, then leans over the railing again. "Don't throw me in," he shouts.

"That should do it."

"Swear to god, if he does..." Muttering to himself, he skips down the stairs and across the lawn to the rocks at the edge of the water. I go inside, to drink some water, to wash my face, to lie down for twenty minutes and stop feeling like the world's spinning too fast.

So much for back to basics.

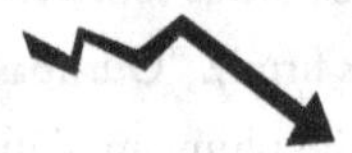

My little rest turns into a solid two-hour nap, but at least I've stopped seeing Highway 6's blacktop unfurl in my mind's eye. Karl and Carter are in the living room, talking softly while Karl sorts jigsaw puzzle pieces on the coffee table.

"Where's Reagan?" I ask as I get myself a glass of water from the open kitchen

"Same as you, asleep," Karl replies, poring over a scatter of blue pieces in the overturned lid of the box.

"It's what all the cool kids are doing." I grab a bag of popcorn and join Carter on the couch. Worrying his upper lip with his teeth, he turns to me before I'm even settled.

"Was it a mistake to invite him?"

"Why do you keep asking that?"

He groans, letting his head fall back. "Do I really have to say it out loud?"

I can guess, but I don't want to. I've seen this on the horizon for hours. Days, maybe. Since Reagan walked in on us talking about him, when he said he doesn't play games. Maybe so, but we sure are. Playing each other, and it's time to lay our cards on the table. "Yeah, actually you do."

"Because he's going to make us fight. Not on purpose, but I keep wanting to lay into Karl, and I realized it's because I'm jealous."

"You should have him," Karl says roughly. "You met him first."

"It's not up to us," I say. "It's his life. We need to maybe deal with the idea that he doesn't want a hook up with any of us."

"What happens if he wants to get with *all* of us?" Carter asks.

I wish I knew. I don't want to damage this friendship. The three of us have come too far together to throw it away for some needy little twink. If only Reagan was so easily dismissed, but the longer he's around us, the more human he's become. "I wish we'd talked about this more before we left Toronto," I say.

"But would you?"

"Share him, you mean? I don't know if I can answer without knowing if he's down for it."

"Hypothetically, though."

I let my head fall back, watching the faint gold tracery of reflected water dance on the cottage's sloped ceiling. I couldn't have shared Pascal, not with anyone. Our relationship had been one of finding the still places within each other and settling there. He is—he was—nothing like Reagan, who burns like cold fire, his energy raw and wild and damn near tangible, imprinted on my senses, lodged in my unguarded heart. To have all of him would ask so much of me. Change everything about my life and how I live it.

"He's a lot," I say as kindly as I can. "He's hot, and hot to go, but I only just found my feet again."

"But if you and him are meant for each other—" Carter starts, his voice cracking with emotion.

"No one is meant for each other," Karl cuts in, glaring up at him from behind the coffee table. "We must not fall prey to such romanticism. Love must be practical as well. So if he ends up with either of you, I won't complain."

"This is ridiculous," Carter replies, rubbing his eyes. "I don't know why I feel anything at all for him. He's so not the kind of guy I even go for."

"Maybe that was your problem," I say, like I've wanted to for years. "You've been going for the wrong guys."

"And he's the right one?"

"You can't know that without giving it a try," Karl says.

"Now, while he's still living with us? If we stop getting along, he's back on the street."

"First, I would not let you do that to him," Karl replies, his gaze unflinching. "Not again. Second, he does have parents, you know."

"Who don't seem to give a shit about him. I've never seen him call them. Do they even know he lost his job?"

"You would have to ask him that."

Carter groans, slumping forward onto his elbows. "It's like some fucking reality show," he mutters.

"The Bachelorette but make it gay as hell?" I suggest.

"Exactly.

"No one said we have to play by the rules."

MARSHMALLOW

REAGAN

THEY'RE TALKING ABOUT ME. I can't hear their words but I feel it in the air like a summer storm. Unless I'm reading too much into Karl's flirting. And the flash of Carter's eyes whenever he does. I retreated to my room in part to break the tension, once it started to remind me of the vibe that year my parents tried to separate. Neither of them could pull the trigger, put themselves and me through the drama of divorce. They just went on being miserable together, speaking less and less, orbiting each other like two black holes, sucking all the goodness out of everything around them.

Stashing this with the other episodes to share with Dr. Whitman when we get back to Toronto, I bounce on the bed a few times so the creaky springs warn the others that I'm awake. When I come out of my room, Karl and Wyn are busy in the kitchen and Carter is on the deck.

By the time I get outside he's down on the lawn, hunched over a blackened hollow in the ground surrounded by rough benches made from split logs. Evening is coming fast, the low sun painting a splash of gold across the still water, the quiet unlike anything I've heard, or

I guess not heard, no sound beyond the whistle of wind through the trees and the buzzing of unseen insects in the grass. I join Carter, who turns out to be starting a fire.

"Can I help at all?" I ask as he stuffs twigs and dried grass into the gaps in the tidy stack of bigger sticks.

"Nope."

"Maybe the guys need a hand."

"They're fine. The kitchen's only so big."

There, they can't say I didn't try to help. "Where'd you learn to do that?"

"Scouts. Plus I start a lot of fires at the smithy."

"The what?"

"The blacksmith's shop. It's part of a maker studio by College. They have a kiln, some welding gear. Heavy equipment that not every artisan can afford."

"So you're a blacksmith too?"

"I'm an apprentice. A pretty half-assed one," he adds under his breath.

"Why do you even want to be a blacksmith?"

"Because I'm an idiot," he says dryly. "I don't know, because it's the only hyper-fixation that I didn't quit in the first six weeks."

"What's a hyper-fixation?"

He glances at me through the first threads of smoke. "You've never heard that? What part of the internet do you hang out on?"

"The shitty one, alright? The one with all the people you'd probably call fascists or something."

"Right. You wouldn't see a lot of neurodivergent content over there. But my socials are a bubble too, I guess. I shut down everyone who comes onto my feed with racist or transphobic comments. Any bullshit, really."

"That must keep you busy, countering all that."

"Fuck countering it," he says with a laugh, fanning the fire with a scrap of cardboard. "I don't even engage. Let them yell at themselves. I hide their comments, or report them if they're abusive, then block the account and move on. Life's too short for me to try educating people through a phone when they've already proved they don't trust the evidence. They're just trolling."

"Can I follow you?"

"You haven't yet?"

"I didn't want to look like a stalker."

"As long as you behave yourself, or I'll block you too."

"How about I just lurk for the first few weeks?" Or months.

"Good idea."

By now the fire is burning hotly, yellow flames leaping from the center of the wood pile. As Carter settles on another bench, the others come to join us, bringing a few bags of chips and an old wooden salad bowl full of grapes. I implement my new policy of keeping my mouth shut right away, accepting a neon green can of some random craft beer from the selection in Karl's cargo pockets then sitting back to watch the three friends in their natural element.

Their friendship is different from everything I've experienced. I've always been competing against the people I thought of as my friends. Even as a kid, we were all chasing the highest marks in the class, the team MVP award, any scrap of validation from the adult world to justify the cages they kept us in.

These three men want nothing from each other. They smile, they laugh, they laugh at each other, but with something I want to call love. Another thing I've probably been wrong about all my life: love, and what it means outside of a family's obligations. I'm meant to love my parents, and I say it to them when I have to, but I can't stand being in a room with them for more than ten minutes.

As for this, I could sit here for hours listening to their stories, even though I miss half the inside jokes and my butt's numb from sitting on a log and mosquitoes dart and dive around my head. Once the fire settles, Carter stacks some rocks around the edge then lays a barbeque grill over the pit. Karl brings out a platter of random things on skewers, with a separate plate for Wyn's vegan stuff, which he lays on the far side of the grill. An act of love, of giving someone what they need without them needing to ask, without it earning you anything.

After weeks of dining in the living room, I've gotten better at eating off my lap. There's something carnal about eating this way, picking the chunks of grilled chicken and veg off the sticks with our teeth, leaning forward so the juices drip onto the ground and not our clothes, then tossing the bare skewers into the fire. Is this actual masculinity? Or is this just real life for a change?

Karl takes the empty trays inside and returns with a grocery bag. He sits beside me and starts handing me the contents: a box of honey graham crackers, a block of chocolate, a bag of marshmallows.

"What's this for?" I ask.

"Have you never had a s'more?"

"A what?"

He looks around at the others. "How do I know what that is and he does not?"

"Maybe because my parents hate fun?"

"Then let me educate you, my friend," he says, clapping his hand on my knee. "Prepare to meet one of the best things you'll ever put in your mouth."

Is he for real? Even Wyn is chuckling as Karl gets up and starts hunting about in the grass by the nearest trees. He shouts in triumph then returns with a couple of skinny branches the length of his arm.

"Can you not tell me what's going on?" I ask as he starts to shred the bark off the end of one of the branches.

"Watch and learn."

Carter is doing the same with a stick of his own. They each impale a marshmallow then hold them over the hot coals

"What does that do?"

"Transmutes mere whipped sugar and gelatin into paradise," Karl says with a grin, the flickering firelight darkening his eyes. "It should be perfect right about...now."

He pulls the thing away from the coals and offers it to me, gooey strands clinging to my fingers as I take it off the end of the stick. It feels both softer and firmer than one from the package, but when I put it in my mouth...

"Oh fuck," I mumble as the lightly crisp exterior gives way to a sugary cloud that coats my tongue. It's sticky and messy and glued to my fingers and I want to eat the whole bag. I look up and the others are watching me over the fire, their eyes glowing. "Sorry, I've never had one of these before. They're really good."

"You've never eaten a marshmallow?" Carter says, fixing another to the end of his stick.

"I wasn't allowed to have a lot of candy growing up. And then I was too scared of getting fat."

"You, fat?"

As he looks me over I cross my arms over my stomach automatically. "I know it's not healthy to think like that. Part of me knew it. But that didn't stop me from shoving my fingers down my throat twice a day...sorry, TMI," I mutter as they recoil, Wyn covering his mouth like I'm making him sick too.

That's why I don't ever tell people. Not then, not now, not ever. Not even at my worst, after that cross country meet in grade 12 when I came second last in the 4000 m because I kept blacking out from low blood sugar. I told everyone I had the flu. Not that I'd scraped my throat raw the night before, after my parents took me to The Keg and I couldn't talk my mom out of ordering me dessert.

"It's okay, Reagan," Karl says, laying his arm more gently around me. "We're all friends here. You're safe."

Safe: easy to say but hard to guarantee. Hard to believe when my whole body is humming with fear. Karl is stroking my back, and I let my breathing follow the steadying rhythm of his touch. Let the silence surround me, the night so still the only sound is the fire and us: the whisper of Karl's palm against my shirt, our mingled breath, our heartbeats.

"I'm going to wash my hands," I say when I stop shaking.

"Let me grab the door for you," Carter says. The darkness is unreal and I let him lead, expecting him to say something about my mini-freak out. But he doesn't. Like he already understands and doesn't need to hear it to know what I'm going through.

I wash my hands in the kitchen sink, a trick I use to avoid going near a toilet. I ate one fucking marshmallow and my body's screaming at me to un-eat it, but that part of my life is over. It has to be. Worn out from the day, from the past week, from being alive, I fuck around the cottage, looking at the shitty décor in detail, adding a couple pieces to Karl's jigsaw puzzle, reluctant to be witness to any more of their joy. They join me soon after and we all head to bed without a lot of talk, leaving me to my endless thoughts.

Thanks, I hate it.

But how can I sleep with all that's on my mind? It's not just the marshmallow but everything: Karl's charm and his swimsuit, Wyn's choices, Carter's caring. What am I meant to do with this much goodness? This much wanting?

But I can't have what I want. Can't turn their friendship into my freak show. There's more than one way to get wrecked. A world of bad behavior I've never been a part of, unless everything I've heard about gay culture is a lie. I could be getting turned inside out right now in the back rooms of some Church St club, or a place like the rear of Wyn's coach house.

Wyn's place, where the three of them can take turns with me, use me how they like, tie me to the X-frame, lock me in that cage. Not just any men, but these men. My men. Greedy little bitch, but right now I'd give anything, any amount of money to make this come true, make me theirs.

I roll onto my stomach, pinning my hard-on against the bed. Like they aren't even mine, my fingers creep into my mouth. I suck, humping the bed, my clothes scraping against my erection, but that's the goddamn point. Make it hurt, make me hate it, make me not want to do it again, because giving in is giving up, because the body is a liar and the mind is its master, all those myths of manhood I once accepted like holy truth. This is the truth, this shuddering need, this helplessness, my own hand gripping the back of my neck to let the rest of me lose control.

I wake up sticky and sore, my fingers still in my mouth. After changing clothes I lie down again, but the moon has shifted and its light pours through the dusty lace curtains, making the foot of the bed glow. A soft, slightly floral printed cloud, and I watch the shifting square of silver light until I can't see anything at all.

BREAKFAST

KARL

THOUGH I WAS YAWNING beside the fire, once I'm in bed sleep escapes me, leaving me adrift on memories of Reagan licking sticky strands of melted marshmallow off his fingers. I wanted to suck it right out of his open mouth, taste him amid the sweetness. Taste him, and I give up my chaste resolution to not fall down this rabbit hole, not imagine what it will be like when he is mine.

Because I do not care if he has a thousand lovers. As long as I'm among them—preferably at the head of the line, but what does it matter when my obsession burns this hot? When the thought of him fucking anyone is as delicious as the thought of him fucking me. In a dozen urgent strokes I'm there, groaning behind my hand as I spill into the other, messing my thighs and picturing his.

I wake to rain drumming softly on the shingles and dampening the air. Cottage life, and not enough to stand between me and coffee. As I pour the first mug Reagan emerges from his room, blinking in the grey light. Huddled in my sweatshirt, he perches on a stool at the kitchen island. I'm about to make an irredeemable joke that will surely ruin myself forever in his eyes when Carter and then Wyn leave their rooms one after the other.

"Ah yeah," Wyn crows, clasping his hands overhead in victory as he spies the rain. "I'll have a big old bowl of I-told-you-so, with a side of this-is-all-your-fault."

"All I can do for you is breakfast at the Y Knot," Carter says.

"Good enough. I'll even drive."

Coffee first, a silent business of clinking spoons and relieved sighs, each man absorbed in his own thoughts. But mine is not the only rumbling stomach and soon we are on the road.

"Where are we going?" Reagan asks me quietly.

"The Y Knot. It's a diner."

"It's called the Why Not?"

"As in the letter y." I mime tying a knot and his face falls. "What's wrong?"

"How am I still alive? I should have wandered into traffic by now. Eighty-five thousand dollars on prep school tuition and I can't even get jokes."

"To be fair, it's not a very good joke."

"The joke's not the point. It's more that my head's so far up my own ass I can't have a normal conversation."

"Maybe you are just hungry. I can't think when I'm hungry." My stomach adds its gurgling agreement. "See? I must fuel the engine."

The Y Knot's hand lettered sign claims the street-front restaurant has been serving peninsula residents and visitors since 1962. I am sure they have not redecorated once in all those years other than to replace a few seat cushions, the paneled walls hung with fishing trophies and black and white photos of Owen Sound, the ceiling brown from the tobacco smoke of decades ago.

Delilah, one of the regular waitresses who looks like she came with the kit with her teetering beehive and a string of pearls around her aged neck, leads us past the locals seated at the bar in their plaid jackets and camouflage to a booth near the window.

"This your first time up here, hon?" she says to Reagan, lavender acrylic nails clacking as she folds her hands around her order pad.

"How did you...I mean, yes," he finishes, sinking low in his seat. "First time."

"You don't say. Coffee all round?"

The younger waitress Sandi brings the coffee, her brown ponytail swishing as she pilots between the tables. Another local person we see every summer, she catches us up on her parents and her dog. As she describes the recent unseasonable appearance of the aurora borealis, Reagan clears his throat.

"I thought we were hungry," he says as she mumbles to a halt.

"Sorry, guys," Sandi says, flipping to a clean page of her pad. "You probably didn't want to hear all that. Did you know what you want to order?"

Reagan asks several bothersome questions: about the cheese in the omelets, the source of the sausages, before deciding on steak and eggs.

"What the hell was that?" Carter hisses as Sandi disappeared into the kitchen.

"What are you talking about?" Reagan asks.

"She was just being friendly."

"Yeah, so she can get a better tip."

"Dude, we've been coming here for ten years. We know her, alright? She's not some faceless drone, she's a person."

"Do you think she actually cares about us?"

"What does that even matter? If she treats us with respect, who cares what's driving her? Are you saying you weren't doing your job for the money?"

"Of course I was, but..." He exhales shakily, his eyes on his paper placemat. "I'll apologize to her."

"Don't make it weird. Just leave a good tip."

"Right. So like twenty percent?"

"Try twenty bucks."

"But my meal was only..." He catches himself and lowers his eyes again. "You're right. I'm sorry."

He doesn't speak again for the rest of the meal, following our chatter but not contributing more than a smile now and then. "Don't worry," I say to him as we're getting back in the car. "Being a whole, conscious person is not a thing you can finish. It is the work of a lifetime."

"Is that why I'm so tired?"

"You're in recovery," Wyn says.

"I was never an addict."

"You were hooked on money, though."

"Oh, if that's what you mean, then yeah. Nailed it."

"Recovery takes time. If you want to sleep, sleep. We'll be able to entertain ourselves."

When we get back he takes Wyn at his word, retreating to his bedroom while the rest of us keep ourselves occupied as one does on a rainy day at the cottage. Carter reads while I work on the puzzle and Wyn does yoga in front of the windows.

"Rain's letting up," he says, standing on one leg as he reaches for the ceiling.

"Will we have those sausages for dinner?" I ask, running through the list of food we've brought.

"How are you hungry already?" Carter asks from behind his book.

"Maybe I just like sausage."

"We knew that, but why do you want to eat again?"

"Very funny."

"Bah dum tiss."

The puzzle pieces have all begun to look the same, and I cover my tired eyes with the flats of my hands. Now all I see is Reagan: the ghost of Reagan, the shadow, shape, smell of him, the heat of his presence, the chill of his absence.

God help me.

"I want to eat because I want to fuck," I groan, "and I can't do the one so I had better do the other."

"Hmm, wonder why that is," Wyn says, folding in half to look at me between his legs.

"You know why, Captain Underpants."

Wyn chuckles, closing his eyes. "You know he's going to be needy. I haven't even touched him and I can already picture him begging for it, twenty-four, seven. I'm getting too old for that shit."

"You'd need a pet sitter," I say.

"Right?" He pivots upright and comes out of his wide stance, shaking his legs. "Someone to take him for walks down the park."

"Feed his hungry little ass," Carter murmured without looking up.

"Hey now," Wyn says with a laugh. "That wasn't in the job description."

Carter snorts. "You're the one who said you were too old for this."

"So is that you volunteering?"

Smirking, he puts the book aside. "No, I'd need at least twenty bucks an hour."

"Can I pay you in Reagan's ass?"

"Sure," he replies, his smile spreading. "I think I'm getting the better end of the deal but—"

"How was your nap?" I say brightly to Reagan, hovering in the doorway to the bedrooms. Biting his lip, Carter disappears behind his book again as Reagan drifts into the room.

"Fine. It's so quiet though. You can hear just about everything."

Carter makes an odd sound, a laugh he turns into a cough as Reagan wanders to the kitchen and opens the fridge. The memory of my mother's voice jerks me from my seat and before long I've mobilized the household, putting Wyn in charge of salad and Carter in charge of drinks and myself in charge of the meat.

"I kind of feel useless," Reagan says, perched on the deck railing near the barbeque. "You guys have a tight system."

"From each according to his ability, to each according to his needs."

"That sounds Communist. I thought your family came to Canada to get away from that stuff."

"Communism was not Croatia's problem. It was greed. Any system that allows the upward concentration of wealth and power will inevitably starve itself. Sometimes it happens on purpose. Desperate people are easier to manipulate."

"No shit. Hello, subprime mortgage industry."

"Interesting."

"Dude, don't tell me you didn't know about that."

"No, I am merely pleased by you embracing vile socialism, my young apprentice."

"Easy there, Obi Wan Bakunin," he says, reaching out his bare foot to prod me with his toe.

"So you did read that essay I sent you."

Corrupting the youth: every old reactionary's favorite pastime. One person's corruption is another's revelation. Reagan had lost so much—to unfettered capitalism and the racist philosophies driving it—that he could have easily become a danger. Bitter, covetous, closeted, eroding his health and well-being out of a man's toxic fear of showing weakness. He had not, and now would not, because I would not let it be so. I would protect him.

The outdoor furniture is still damp from the morning's rain and we eat standing around the barbeque in an odd cluster as if we're at a party with not enough chairs. I don't know what Carter and Baldwin said to one another inside but every time someone opens their mouth, they tense. Every bite seems to matter, eyes following hands as they raise towards a mouth, watching the movement of the throat as the man swallows. The man: Reagan, looking from one to the other of us with growing suspicion.

"I don't mean to be rude or nothing," he says at last, toying with a forkful of salad, "but I thought you guys didn't fuck each other."

"Why would you think we did?" Wyn asks, his eyes evasive.

"Something's up. The body language is fucking pornographic."

"Do you believe in love?" Carter asks him. "I mean really believe in it?"

"I don't know," Reagan says, resting his plate on the broad top rail of the deck. "People sure seem to think it's real."

"But do you?"

"I said I don't know. What's going on?"

"Nothing. I just wonder what it is you think keeps people together. Beyond money, beyond kids. If everyone had perfect choice, would people still fall in love?"

"You're talking about it like love makes sense. But if love wasn't part of the equation, we'd never fall for the wrong people. Or for more than one person at once."

"Love makes you make bad choices?"

"Not that so much as it makes every choice more complicated. It's not just you, it's everyone you have to account for. Your choices affect other people."

"Everyone's choices affect other people."

"Duh, because they exist in the world. But when you love someone, you see the effects close up. Your choices are right there in your face, every day."

As he turns to gaze across the water the clouds thin, then separate, drenching him in golden sunlight and making him narrow his eyes. A wild young man on the cusp of his future, and I want to gather him into my arms, protect him from all that is to come, in the way one wishes to save another from one's own fate.

THE PEAK

CARTER

WHILE KARL STAYS OUTSIDE to clean the grill, the rest of us tidy the kitchen. Most of the food we bring up here needs little preparation and we're done quickly, the few dishes washed, the leftover sausages and the rest of Wyn's mushroom skewers in the fridge.

"It's a nice night," Wyn says as he wipes the island countertop. "We could go up to the peak and catch the moon."

"You want me to climb a mountain in the dark?" Reagan asks, wrinkling his nose.

"There's an easy trail. And it's not a mountain, just a hill."

"Is it legit?" Reagan asks me as Wyn goes to his room to get his headlamp.

"Do you not like the dark?" I don't want to ask if he's afraid, don't want to force his fears to the surface. Plenty of men take that as an attack, and he's already on edge, worrying at his cuffs, his eyes wide.

"You know how it goes, hazing the new guy," he says with a false smile.

"No one here cares about that macho bullshit. We're not going to throw you in the lake or leave you behind or anything. Honest. Why, did that happen to you?"

"Not a lake. But yeah. I don't know if you played a lot of sports in high school."

"I was a bit of a gym rat but no, I didn't play hockey or anything."

He exhales unsteadily, his hands twisting together. I want to wrap my arms around him and tell him everything is going to work out. That things are going to get better, that his past doesn't matter and his future is bright, as long as he doesn't give up. I can't prove any of these things, and false hope is crueler than none at all, but I can't leave him like this. "If you ever want to talk about it, you can talk to me. Or Dr. Whitman, that's what he's there for."

Swallowing hard, he nods, hiding his hands in his sleeves. Trying to hide how he feels, his shoulders hunched, whole body rigid and I can't take it anymore and I reach for him and he goes into my arms. He's shaking, like a wild thing chased by dogs, burrowing his face into the hollow of my shoulder as I hold him tight, breathing in the scent of him. But this isn't lust, it's care. I care about this self-tormenting young man and his starving heart.

"I never believed that kindness made a difference," he sniffles against my chest. "Co-operation's for suckers, right? For losers who can't make it on their own. All that matters is that you win. And it's bullshit. Everything I am is based on that lie. And now that I don't believe it, I don't know what I am. Like I threw away the map and now I'm lost."

"You're not lost. I've got you."

"Yeah, but now what? I don't mean to boast, but I'm not wrong, am I? If you all weren't such good friends I'd be a real problem for you."

I sigh, nuzzling into his hair, so soft now he's given up the gelled look. I want him in a way that makes all other wanting hollow. Like all my other relationships were shadows of this feeling, like fate brought him to me so I could learn how to forgive. "Reagan, I'm not going to make you choose between us. If I'm not who you're meant to be with, then so be it. I'd rather see you happy than make you miserable."

"But what if it's the choice that's making me miserable? I don't want to hurt any of you. But I don't know if I can deal with being around you and not wanting you. All of you. Seriously, I've never wanted a contest to end with everyone winning. I guess that's not possible, no matter how woke everyone thinks they are. It's human nature to be jealous."

"I don't believe that," I say loosening my hold so I look him in the eye. "Without co-operation, without community, what are we? Lonely naked apes. Cucumbers with anxiety. We don't need each other because we're human, we're human because we need each other. Like I need you, Reagan."

"You shut up," he murmurs, trembling in a whole new way. "Don't break my little heart."

"Let's talk about it later."

Clinging to my arms, he nods urgently, his dick bumping against my thigh. Alone, I'd have him naked and propped on the kitchen island by now, but Wyn wants to go on his damn walk, and it's probably for the best. We need to take this slowly. Learn how Reagan fits into my life. Our lives, because I won't make him choose between the three of us. I want him to have every happiness, every chance to discover himself.

If he doesn't explode first, his nails biting into my biceps as he shivers. "What do you need, little rabbit?" I ask softly.

He whimpers, shoving his face into my shoulder again. "Why is this so hard?" he breathes.

"You never get what you don't ask for."

"Then will you kiss me?"

I would have found a way to be happy being just his friend, watching him become the man he's meant to be. The chance to be more is too much to resist. Like this is the natural outcome of that one bad decision we both made, fumbling in the dark. Like this is my chance to apologize for exploiting him when he was so vulnerable, but if I'd done any different—tried to reason with him or told him to get fucked—I'd have lost him forever. The fact that he's here with me now, well, I can't call it fate or destiny. I don't know that those things exist, or if they're just the stories we tell ourselves after we've made a choice. But it means something; he means something to me, both for the person he is and for the person he makes me want to be.

So much to say, but then I wouldn't be able to kiss him. So much to say tomorrow, because right now there is the feel of his cheek against the palm of my hand, the soft rasp of stubble and the soft skin of youth. There's his little gasp as I slip my hand under his chin to raise his face to mine. There are his lips, trembling under mine, then the tremor that passes down his spine as those lips open in surrender.

Like that blow job, he barely knows what to do. I don't care, I'm not here for a skills contest, I just want to possess him. Taste him deeply, feel him suck at my tongue like he sucked my dick, hard and messily. Hear him groan deep in his throat as I squeeze his pretty little ass, feel his whole body shake against me. What he doesn't know, I'll teach him. Whatever he wants, I'll do. Repeatedly and until he's mine for good, but when I pull back my heart drops at the sight of the tears gathering on his pale lashes.

"What's wrong?"

He shakes his head, the tears scattering like diamonds, his mouth pressed shut. "Tell me what you want, Reagan."

"I don't know what I want," he breathes. He burrows into the hollow of my shoulder again, as if he can escape something that's coming from inside him, and as much as I long to protect him, there are times when we all need to be challenged.

"I think you know exactly what you want," I say, pulling him close to my chest. "You just don't know if you're allowed to want it."

He shudders, his hands knotted in my shirt. "How do you know so much about me?" he murmurs.

"I've spent a lot of time thinking about you."

His head jerks up. "You have not."

"Why wouldn't I? It's incredible, watching you change before my eyes, becoming your own person, not that cardboard cut-out of a man."

"Becoming a slut, you mean," he says, wiping his eyes.

"If that's what you want to call yourself. But I'd like you to be *my* slut. And I have to say, it's getting me pretty hot, thinking about watching you get railed. Letting another man use your sweet mouth."

He shudders again, a little moan escaping his closed lips. I want them open, want his mouth full of my cock, but I can't push him in this moment of fragility, when our whole future is being decided.

"Okay," he creaks, "but your friends? Really?"

"I wouldn't trust just anyone with you, bunny. I'd make you *our* slut."

"Ooh..." I'm beginning to love that shiver, the way his body vibrates against mine. "Don't you think you'll be jealous?" he asks.

"That's not your problem to solve. It's mine. I know I don't the best track record, but if it's what you need, I'm willing to try. Couples fight, Reagan. They argue about all sorts of shit, but that doesn't have to mean the end of their relationship."

"What about the others?"

"I can't speak for them."

"Do you mean I have to have this conversation again?" he groans, sagging in my arms. "Oh shit, twice?"

"Maybe not right now."

"No, first you're going to make me climb a fucking mountain in the dark."

We find the others smoking weed on the deck, Karl bouncing with eager excitement. It's late enough the mosquitoes have settled down as we start up the well-worn trail to the north of the cottage, following the bobbing beam of Wyn's headlamp. Neither of the others say anything about the fact that Reagan sticks to me, though Wyn had to see us hugging in the cottage.

I soon stop thinking about them, my attention bouncing back and forth between trying not wreck my ankles and wonderment at the moonlit landscape. This is why so many of us drag our asses up here from the city every summer weekend, why people mortgage their houses to buy a cottage, because there's no substitute for the feeling of being in a forest. Of breathing air that's being made for you right then and there by every living thing you see. Immersed in the rustle of the leaves as if the leaves were part of you, as if you were part of the forest.

We become our ancestors when we go among the trees, almost without trying, and tonight is no exception, the four of us struck by silent awe as we pass from dark to silver moonlight to dark again. Time seems to slow, familiar landmarks passing unseen in the night as we climb the trail. Breathing hard through his nose, Reagan has fallen behind and I stop to wait for him.

"I made a chart earlier," he says as I switch on my flashlight.

"A chart?"

"How else was I supposed to compare you guys?"

"And?"

"And I don't know. Maybe I'm greedy, but there was no way to pick just one. You're all so different." His toe catches and he stumbles forward, catching himself against me. "Fuck, am I ever out of shape."

"It's not much further."

It still seems to take another hour before we come out of the thinning forest and onto the broad plateau. False trails lead away from the rocky platform, which looks out across the lake towards the south, giving an open view of the clear night sky, though even here the stars are thin thanks to a few million people's light pollution. It doesn't matter, there's beauty enough, of the kind that makes you stop and stare, like we do, gawking about like we've never seen the place, though climbing here is one our group's rituals.

Though the air is still at the lake's edge, the wind is stronger this high up, tugging at our clothes and hair and making Reagan shiver. Standing beside him, Karl puts his arm around his waist and pulls him close as they gaze out across the moonlit water. I watch them, waiting for that twist in my guts, that fear that I'm being outflanked, discarded. And yet Karl means the world to me. He's been my friend through some of my worst times. Wyn as well, and nothing could make me hurt him after what he's gone through, losing his partner so suddenly and horribly. I'd give—I have given—them anything they needed: love, money, food, a home. This chance, if it's what they want too.

Karl and Reagan are talking softly, leaning into one another. Wyn is sitting cross legged on a shelf of rock, his eyes half closed in meditation. I'm about to join him when Karl suddenly jerks away from Reagan.

"You little flirt," he murmurs.

"But would you?" Reagan says, standing so close to him their shadows are one shadow.

"What's he want?" Wyn asks, though he hasn't moved.

"We have ourselves a hungry little bunny. He doesn't think one cock will be enough for him."

Wyn's eyes flick open. "Is that so? You want to weigh in on this, Carter?"

"I'm game."

He unfolds from his pose and gets to his feet. "As long as you know I don't do one night stands," he says to Reagan. "And I don't do tourists."

Reagan whispers something to Karl, who lets him go. Licking his lips, he crosses the narrow plateau, the wind flattening his sweatshirt against his body as he approaches Wyn and carefully takes his hand.

Wyn pulls him closer, threading his other hand through Reagan's soft hair. Whispers something that makes him nod enthusiastically. Smiles, then kisses him, a strong, possessive kiss that makes Reagan's knees buckle as Wyn's tongue delves deep into his willing mouth. It's raw and sensual and something tells me to look away, but if we weren't all open to this then it wouldn't be happening. We all understand consent. If they want privacy, we'll let them have it.

Instead we have this show, Reagan's fair skin gleaming in the moonlight, Wyn a beast of shadows writhing around him. Beside me, Karl makes some incoherent sound between a hum and a moan. I wouldn't make much more sense if I tried speaking, my brain puddling somewhere in my shoes, leaving my dick in charge. And it wants this. Wants to know what happens next, what he'll do next, this man I should never have met.

What he does is loosen his arms from Wyn's neck. When Wyn lets go he steps away and into Karl's embrace

Look, I'm pretty vanilla. I don't watch my friends fuck. And yes, I've seen Karl kiss someone, at a club, at a party. He's never kissed like this, like Reagan is his prey, pinning Reagan's head between his hands, lapping and biting at his lips, while Reagan's hips snap and thrust, denied contact with Karl's body by the strength of his grip. Lost to everything but each other, their stumbling feet send a few stones shooting towards the edge of the plateau. Wyn sees it too.

"Hey, let's go back to the cottage, you two. We've got the rest of the week to play with our new pet."

By the time we reach home we're all yawning. "Never mind," I say, ruffling Reagan's hair as his puppy-dog eyes watch Wyn and Karl disappear into their rooms. "We'll all still be here in the morning. Come, sleep with me."

"But you just said—"

"Just to sleep. I want you near me."

Pink-faced, he follows me to the bathroom to brush our teeth, then into my room. I leave my t-shirt on so he knows I'm serious about not fooling around. We have time to spare. All the time in the world, because this is only the beginning.

In bed I pull him close, curling around his back, ignoring the press of his ass against my misbehaving dick. Reagan is determined not to be ignored, however, rocking his hips with growing intent. I wrap my hand around his jaw and turn his head to face me. "Are you trying to get in trouble?"

"Why, is that an option?"

"You're right, you are a slut."

"As long as I'm your slut."

I can't help it, and I fall on him, kissing him awkwardly over his shoulder. Anything to taste him, mark him, own him.

"Carter," he gasps as I scrape my teeth across his throat.

"What do you need?"

"You know what I need."

"Your mouth full of my cock?"

He replies with a moan and another tremor, and it's what I want too, but not like the first time. Not towering over him as he kneels and lets me have him. I want him to work harder for it. Earn my come, if he wants it that bad. Learn what I like so he can do it again. I roll to my back and he flips over, drinking in the sight of me as I hitch my briefs off my hips, letting my erection fall heavily against my stomach and earning another moan from Reagan, but when I reach for him he scrambles off the bed.

"I want to see you," he says, pushing open the faded curtains and bathing me in moonlight. A stark portrait in black and white, all bare skin and shadow, and he stands by the window to savor it, his panting breath the only sound beyond the pounding of my heart.

TEASE

REAGAN

SO MUCH HAS HAPPENED so quickly that I need a moment for my brain to catch up to my body. The first time I did this, I was drunk. So drunk that the memory barely exists. What's left is a patchwork of sensations: the hard sidewalk under my knees, the ache of my throat as he thrust deep, the way his pubes tickled my nose. I woke up under a bush in Christie Pits, two and a half kilometers away, shirtless and sticky and scared.

Not so scared that I didn't want to do it again, but now that my chance has come, it feels too important to rush. I need to know that this isn't just a fantasy that should never come true, that it's what I really want. Carter waits in silence, except for the brush of his palm over his naked skin, a sensual slither that draws me to him one shaking step at a time.

I climb onto the bed on the dark side, leaving his body exposed to the silver light. As I lean in he pulls me to him for a last messy kiss, leaving my lips wet. He's all I can smell, and I let that lure me further down the bed until I'm crouching between his thighs.

"God, Reagan..." he groans, his eyes rolling closed as I encircle the base of his cock with my hand. He's mine in this moment, so desperate for me that I could make him do anything. But what's the fun of that? I can't make myself act like I'm in charge when what I want is to be owned.

His girth filling my hand, I work his foreskin past the fat head. Everything is him: the sound of his heaving breath, the musky scent that clings to my tongue, the inescapable sight of his real and present cock here in my hand, waiting for my mouth.

"Please, Reagan," Carter gasps, knotting his hands in the bedsheet. "Don't tease me like this."

As if his command was what I needed to go on, I stroke my tongue around the glistening head, gathering the salted droplet welling from his slit. We moan in unison as I do it again, and then my last fears disintegrate as he sets his hand on the back of my head, the weight of his touch altering the balance, making it clear who rules who. I want to be his pet. Their pet, if that's what they all agree. Want to give myself to making them happy, spend my days being good. Being wanted.

The way he wants this, his hips rising to meet me as I lick him up and down, now and then taking the thick head in my mouth. The flex of his grip in my hair tells me to keep going. Deeper and deeper, his hand not forcing me but not letting me stop, until my nose is buried in his hair and his cock is buried in my throat. He thrusts, shoving even deeper, testing my limits, but I have no limits. This is what I wanted, this overwhelming force, this decadence of serving another man on my knees, his every penetration sending waves of sharp pleasure through the center of me. All that education, those years of good behaviour, of driving myself to be what I thought a man should be, and this is what it bought me: a cock in my mouth, a hand on my head, my surrender.

"Fuck, bunny, I'm not going to last," Carter pants as I suck him. "Tell me where you want my come. Down your throat? Or all over your pretty face."

I moan around him, pushing back for the first time against his stern grip so he'll let me sit up, hoping like hell he understands.

"That's what I thought."

As I lift my head he grabs me by the hair again, holding me in place as he strokes himself urgently. In a few seconds he's there, groaning deeply as his hot come strikes my cheek, my open mouth, the shock of it igniting an explosion in my balls, a quivering, spurting sensation that might as well be an orgasm. It's not like when I jerk off alone but infinitely stronger, like it's Carter's come that spurted from me. Like this is a baptism that makes me his forever.

He cleans my face—with his own shorts, I think, because the soft cloth smells like his cock. My own jocks are glued to me because, yes, once again, someone creaming my face has made me come without anyone touching me. Murmuring about house-training horny little rabbits, Carter undresses me and mops me up and tucks me into bed beside him, where I fight the need to ask to do it all again until I am asleep. For all the things I've obsessed about, I could do worse.

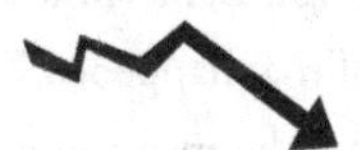

I wake up with a bounce as Carter springs out of bed. Someone is blowing a trumpet in the living room, playing that fucking army song. Swearing worse than I've ever heard him, Carter yanks on sweatpants and storms out of the room.

"I swear to fucking God, Karl—"

The noise ends as abruptly. "So you're up."

"I wonder why."

"Because it's a beautiful day and you can't waste it in bed. No matter how much fun you're having."

By now I'm fully awake. Wearing Karl's campfire-scented sweatshirt and nothing else, I dip to the bathroom where I scrub with cold water and a lot of grumbling. I'm brushing my teeth when someone knocks.

"Are you in the shower?" Carter asks

"Showers are an option?"

"Don't shave your legs or nothing," he says with a laugh, "but yeah, you can have a shower."

Which I do, and it's glorious, though I keep it brief, fighting a creeping sense that last night was a dream. Not being with Carter but what came before, when I climbed a mountain in the dark then kissed three different men. The bathroom seems unreal, hollow like a movie set, and I wriggle back into Karl's sweatshirt and leave before it gets any weirder.

Dressed, I head to the kitchen, following the smell of coffee. As I reach for a cup I feel warmth on the back of my legs. Two hairy arms encircle me, one hand sliding up under my shirt, the other down to graze over my sudden erection.

"Good morning, my little zečić" Karl purrs, planting a kiss on my cheek as I lay my head back against his shoulder with a shudder of relief

"I was so scared none of that happened."

"It happened. I'd like it to happen some more." My mouth floods as he prods my backside with his erection.

"Save it for later," Wyn chuckles beside us as Karl nips me on the neck then lets me go. "Where's my sugar, bunny?"

My heart skipping, my balls throbbing, I go to him, kissing him hard like I did last night, so he knows that I mean it, his strong hands kneading my back as I grind against him.

"Easy, boy. It's going to be a long day, you ought to save your strength."

"He's not joking," Carter says, wandering past rubbing sunblock on his nose.

"I didn't think he was."

"If you want this candy, you better earn it," Wyn says, unhooking my arms from around his neck. "And have some breakfast. I'm not carrying your ass home if you get worn out by this hike."

"Hike?"

"It's not that hard," Carter says, handing the sunblock to Wyn. "Like last night."

"Except I'll be able to see where I'm going? Sign me the fuck up, guys."

"Or you can just chill here if you want. No pressure," Wyn says, rubbing the white cream into his cheeks.

As if I'm going to bench myself. "I'm good. As long as there's no bears and shit."

As I say this, something hairy strokes the back of my neck. Despite being indoors and therefore extremely safe from bears, or coyotes, or any of the things crawling through the forest that might want to eat my face, I scream like a little bitch, leaping away from Karl, who's laughing as he waves his broad, hairy hand.

"Fuck you, man! Don't creep up on me."

"I'm sorry," he says with a guilty grimace. "But at least we know your reflexes are good."

I'm still simmering as we pile into the 4x4. I've never seen a prank that didn't lead to another, and sitting behind him I suppress my urge to get revenge with a wet willy. Which would only escalate things, earning me something worse.

It's a short drive, just long enough for me to doubt everything I thought I'd figured out. Because none of this makes sense. A few months ago, I was a hundred percent sure I was hetero. And I was kind of indifferent to sex. Now that I've decided I'm gay, I want to fuck every man in arm's reach. Like all the stereotypes are true, and gay men really are sluts: hypersexual, consequence-free. Unless that's all in my head and I'm doing gayness wrong, another male benchmark I'll never meet. Because what man wants to be at someone else's mercy? Only a slutty little bottom like me who doesn't know any better, who catches feelings for every guy who gives me attention.

Or maybe not. Maybe this really does mean something. All of these men are so confident, so rooted in themselves, immune to the sort of insecurities that haunt me. Sexually dominant, but not forceful. If all they wanted was to bang me, they could have had me any time. Instead they've made me part of their circle, brought me to their special place, given me the choice.

My head buzzing, I climb out of the truck, then follow the others from the small gravelly lot along a narrow track up a little hill and suddenly all my thoughts stop, because I have never seen anything so enchanting.

We're standing on a rise above a pebbled beach at the head of an inlet. Beyond, the open lake glitters in the pearly sunshine, but in this secluded glade all is soft and cool, shaded by the overarching trees, their lower branches dipping into the still water. Birds hop along the narrow beach, and when I step on a branch, the thick brown body of a forest animal plops into the green-brown depths from its hiding spot on the bank. A simple beauty, made of rustling leaves and solitude. Every other place I've been that might have outranked it as a tourist attraction has been full of, well, tourists. This feels personal, a place no one else knows, a secret they've shared with me, without my asking or deserving.

No one is in a hurry to go anywhere, each of them wandering alone in the same state of holy wonder, but when Wyn sets out along a path leading into the trees, I follow him. Hearing me, he stops to wait, and the two of us walk in single file until we reach the headland. More beauty, and without a word we sit down on a silvered log set near the water's edge, no doubt for this very reason.

Breathing slowly, his hands loose on his knees, Wyn closes his eyes. I do the same, letting the wind and the warmth of the sun and the soft sound of the water rippling against the stony shore take my mind away. What does it matter if I'm broke, if I'm broken? If this happiness passes and leaves me in pain? The sun will still shine, the water still speak, as it always has, as it always will. The only things you can trust in the world, the only things that endure.

"I see why you like this place so much," I say once I'm sure my voice won't break from the feelings coursing through me.

"This is sacred space," he murmurs without opening his eyes. "This is how I charge my batteries."

"Thank you for bringing me here."

"Anytime. You need more of this in your life, bunny."

"Is that it for me? I'm a rabbit forever?"

Grinning, he opens his eyes. "It's a compliment," he says, stretching his arms before him. "Rabbits are fast, they're determined, they can't be stopped. They bring luck."

"If you cut their foot off."

He laughs, sliding his arm around me. "What would you like to be called?"

"I don't really mind," I say, resting my head on his warm shoulder. "I guess it could be worse."

"You sure?"

"I'd rather be a bunny than a pussy."

He laughs again, shaking me. "Come on, let's keep walking. There's even more to see."

THE CHASE

WYN

HE MIGHT BE CARRYING a lot of trauma, but at least Reagan's easy to train. All I had to do was sit still and he followed my lead. We'll unlock the man behind his masks in time. For now I'll enjoy the sight of his pale thighs and the occasional flash of his ass from beneath his silky running shorts as he climbs the trail ahead of me. I've known the property owner Iain longer than I've known both Carter and Karl, and he keeps the land maintained like a first class conservation area, with fresh blazes on the trees to mark the route. Fallen logs lie to either side where they've been dragged off the trail, which rises and falls over the old fingers of dolomite that thrust into the lake.

There's a map of the property hanging in the cottage, and between that and being up here so often, both with and without the guys, that the trails are embedded in my muscle memory. A few times I've been up here late at night with Iain and his circle to play hide and seek. With a twist, because Iain's the biggest freak I know. I wouldn't play like that these days, trusting my body and my health to some masked stranger, who more often than not was someone I'd dated before. Yet I can't stop my dick from twinging as we reach the open meadow where the hunt would usually begin. Near the center stands one of the most interesting features of the property, a bower of grape vines that Iain's trained into a sort of gazebo nearly ten feet high.

"This is some Zelda shit," Reagan murmurs as we pass under the leafy arch into its rustling cool. "This didn't grow like this, right?"

"Nah. Iain's been shaping it for years. Used to be a ring of sticks in the mud."

"It's really special. Like everything here. I'm honored that you want to show me."

"I'm glad you're here to see it." I catch his hand and slowly draw him near, slowly kiss him. His mouth tastes like coffee and skin, his eager whimpering making my balls ache. But when I cup his ass he freezes, and I lift my head.

"What's on your mind, bunny?"

He smirks, looking up through his pale lashes. "I've been wondering about all that stuff in your place, behind the wall. And if you ever use any of it."

"Sometimes."

His coy smirk vanishes. "Really?" he squeaks, as if he didn't expect a genuine answer.

"Kink isn't just for white billionaires, you know."

"That wasn't what I was thinking."

"You're thinking that you want to find out what it's like?"

Pressing against me, he takes a deep shuddering breath and lets it out slowly. "I mean...if you ever wanted to show me," he murmurs hoarsely.

"I can show you right now."

"How?" he asks, glancing about like there's a flogger hanging from the branches.

"I don't need props to run you," I say, catching his chin so he's centered on me. "I promise, I can make you nut without laying a hand on you."

The wall of woven vines creaks as I push him back against it. Next time I'll rope him to it, but for now my words will do.

"You're going to show off for me, rabbit. Start with putting your fingers in your mouth. Good boy," I purr as he shoves two stiffened fingers into his mouth. "Now close those pretty lips around them and suck. Suck like you wish you were sucking me. You're going to be so pretty when you're choking on my dick."

He moans around his thrusting fingers, his eyes rolling back. He's losing focus too soon when I want him to feel my command. "Stop."

With a slurp he pulls his wet fingers out of his mouth. Damn that mouth, and I almost wish I'd taken his offer that night he stayed with me. This is better, now that we trust each other more. Now that I know he wants this and isn't offering because he feels like he owes me. "Do you want more?"

Swallowing hard, he nods. "I know all about red light, green light, too. I know."

"In that case, show me, Reagan. Show me your cock. Show me how hard you are for me. Show me how much you want me."

He cries out, face contorted like he's in the midst of orgasm. I slow my breathing, slowing the pace, bringing us both back to level as he tugs down his shorts, then raises the bulky sweatshirt to show off his dripping cock.

"Nice. Almost makes me want to change my mind. But I want to give you something to look forward to. The day when I put my hands on you and make you mine. Now show me how you stroke yourself. Let me see you come for me." I'm about to nut just watching him as he starts to pump his hand, his hips rising to meet each stroke.

"Fingers, Reagan. In your mouth." He does it, shoving his fingers deep then pulling them nearly out. Again, teasing me and himself, his other hand slowing to match his slurping rhythm. Until his need is too strong, his eyes closing again as he humps into his own hand, sucking hard at his fingers, his movements shaking the bower the way watching him shakes me. But before my self-control gives way he comes, stifling his shout with his thrusting fingers as he spurts onto the forest floor.

His hand slowly drops from his mouth as he falls back against the wall of vines. Stepping around the dusty droplets, I move up beside him, craving another taste of his mouth, his trembling lips.

"Did I do it right?" he slurs as I pull back from our kiss so he can catch his breath.

"It was perfect."

With the pack of wipes in my day pack I help him clean up. "We can keep walking if you want," I say as we leave the bower.

"There's more?"

"There's always more."

"I wouldn't know, I don't spend a lot of time in the great outdoors."

"You've never gone camping?" I ask as we return to the trail.

"Just the once. I was too busy with tennis. And lacrosse, and SAT classes, and track and field and all the other stuff my parents put me in so they didn't have to spend time with me." He drops behind me as the trail narrows, winding between a patch of fragrant cedars. Similar trails run all over the property, threading through the trees and winding around boulders, crossing each other in an irregular patchwork. I stop where the ridge gives a view of the meadow from the other side of the bower. Standing beside me, he hugs his arms as he gazes back at the little structure, not speaking until I lead him onward.

"Were you always a jock?" he asks.

"I don't think I'm a jock now."

"Dude, you're a fitness influencer."

"That doesn't make me a jock. I spend too much damn time marketing. And editing, and so much other shit."

"I guess it's tougher than it looks."

"Almost everything is. I don't know how much longer I'll keep the channel. I need to make up my mind soon."

"About what?"

"Everything. What I'm going to do for the second half of my life. I don't want to do this forever." I stop, so abruptly that he walks into me, but that's okay, I want him close, and I turn and catch his elbow before he steps back. "Don't think that I include you in that. You, I want to keep."

He doesn't reply, ducking his head to avoid my eye, his hands balled to fists. Maybe I pushed him too hard. Made him accept too much. "I'd like to know what you're thinking," I say. "You don't have to tell me but—"

"Am I normal?" he blurts. "I mean, people don't just do this. Fall for three people at once and jerk off in a tree hut. This is crazy, right?"

"It's unusual but I don't think it's crazy. I don't really like throwing that word around anyway."

"Why do I want it, though? What's making me do this?"

"I don't know. But you don't need to be afraid. We all want the best for you. If you want to just be friends—"

"That's not it at all. I want you, all of you. But doesn't that make me the worst kind of person?" he pleads. "That I can't make up my mind?"

"You have made up your mind, though. It's the rest of the world that's telling you that you can't have what you want. It's sure not me."

"This doesn't bug you? The thought that I'm not all yours?"

"I don't own you, Reagan. No one does. If you choose to share part of yourself with me, I'll take it as the blessing that it is. But I can't control you. No one can."

He exhales shakily, his shoulders dropping. "Wow. Autonomy kind of sucks."

"Good job, you're now an existentialist."

"Ugh, another fucking label? You people and your identities."

"*You people* now includes you, gay boy."

"But I'm not…fuck." He drops his head to my chest, clinging to me desperately. "I hate this so much. Not knowing who I am."

"It'll pass."

I hold him as he rides the wave of his emotions. Coming out is about so much more than how other people see you. What matters most is how you start to see yourself. If he's been closeted all his life, he's got work to do to unpack his history. The work starts now.

At last he's breathing quietly again, his head resting in the hollow of my shoulder, his arms loosened from their death grip around my waist. He lifts his head with a shy smile that looks like it needs a kiss, but as I bend to him the bushes beside us start to shake. We disentangle in a hurry and back away, Reagan's face white with fear, even though we'd have smelled a bear long before.

The bushes part and out stumbles Karl, twigs and leaves stuck to his beard. "Boo!" he says, waggling his fingers like claws.

"Goddamn it, Karl, don't do that shit. Trail's right there."

Brushing debris off his shirt, he sticks out his tongue at me. "You're no fun. And you," he says to Reagan. "From the way you nearly ran for your life, you must really be a rabbit."

"Said the bear," Reagan replies dryly.

"Bah dum tiss. Aren't you scared I'm going to eat you?"

"Not eat, exactly. And seriously, is that it? Everyone's in on it, and I'm a fucking rabbit for the rest of my life?"

"A fucking rabbit? Sounds terrific. When can we start?" Grinning, he snatches at Reagan, who skips out of his reach with a laugh.

"I thought we already had started." Karl lunges and he dodges again.

"Run all you like, rabbit. I'll still catch you."

"Then what?"

"I'd sink my claws deep. Make you beg for mercy."

"Seriously, what happens if you catch me?" he asks, his eyes full of fire.

Karl rises from his hunting crouch. "That I don't know. Perhaps I'll want what you gave Carter."

Glancing at me, Reagan laughs. "Is that all?"

"You were in a hurry that night, as I was told. Here, there's no one to sneak up on us. I could take my time. Or rather, you could." Throughout his speech, Karl advances on Reagan, who retreats one hesitant step at a time.

"Good luck catching me," he says with a smug little grin I want to fuck into oblivion.

"You can't hide from me, rabbit. I'd smell you anywhere. Smell your fear."

"I'm not afraid of you." Yet he can't hide the shake in his voice.

"You should be."

With that he lunges at Reagan, who shrieks in terrified glee and takes off like the proverbial rabbit, disappearing down the trail in seconds.

"Well? Get going, Smokey," I say to Karl.

"You take the western branch. We'll pin him near the creek."

"Oh, I'm part of this now?"

"Are you telling me you don't feel like hunting a slut?"

"When you put it that way..." Who could say no? My dick is already rising again, like a dog to the hunter's horn. We're going to chase him, and we're going to catch him, and then we're going to eat him up.

THE CATCH

REAGAN

IF I STOP TO think about what I'm doing, they'll catch me. All I can do is run.

The paths crisscross, meeting at open glades, sometimes with a fire pit in the middle. If I can get back to the car park I'll call it a win, but I don't care if I lose. I'm playing to lose.

That doesn't mean I won't make them work for the win. And trust me, they're going to have to work hard. I might have mentioned being on the track and field team in school, but I know I didn't tell anyone about running cross-country. A brutal sport to foist on kids, but I felt more joy on those grueling runs than at any other time in school. Just me and the sky and the ground under my feet, the other runners barely present, time seeming both infinite and non-existent.

Once or twice since then I've felt the same high: the first time my crypto account broke half a million, a couple of really good jerk-off sessions when I made myself wait for hours. This is already edging that sensation, my skin prickling, all my senses alive. Waiting to hear their footsteps. A snapping branch, a squawking bird, a sign, but beyond my own heavy breathing the forest is quiet.

Trusting the downward slope of the landscape to direct me towards the lake and the parking lot, I run at a quick but sustainable pace, following the closest thing to a straight path and crossing several of the little openings in the trees. The paths seem made for running, and maybe they are, if we aren't the first people to use that fairy tree for sex. That was all of ten minutes ago. Now I'm running through a forest like I'm being chased by zombies, trying to prolong the time between now and when Karl and Wyn...

My knees buckle and I stumble to a halt. Now's as good a time as any to check my six, catch my breath, plan my next move. Treading softly, I creep along the tunnel of the trail to the open space ahead, though I don't stop there to rest. As I start down the trail opposite I see a flash of Wyn's white shirt, moving among the trees in the hollow below me. I drop into a crouch behind a prickly bush that doesn't do a whole lot to hide me as I scan the rest of the forest.

I retreat, but there's only one more trail leading away from this clearing. I've barely ran a hundred meters when I hear a piercing whistle from my left. Skidding to a stop, I see Karl picking his way down a tumble of lichen-stained rocks. His sharply rising whistle is answered by Wyn from behind the ridge to my right as he moves to intercept me.

They're hunting me with purpose. Hunting me...

A thrill rips through my body as I realize that makes me prey. I bolt, giving up on secrecy in favor of speed, pouring everything I've got into outpacing them. Another clearing beckons at the bottom of this slope but as I reach it Carter steps out from another trail, his arms wide, his smile ravenous.

Who fucking told him? Who fucking cares? What matters is getting away from him, and in an act of gymnastics I'll never repeat, I spin in midstride and take off back up the hill, pursued by the sound of his laughter.

I don't care. I don't care what I look like, if they think I'm a simp or a pussy, if this fear makes me less of a man. All I can think of is getting away, making this hard for them, making them regret their offer. At the next clearing I make a scrambling hairpin turn and start down the adjacent trail. To put them off my tail and give my screaming legs a break after that uphill sprint.

I'm feeling confident until I reach the creek. It's not much of a creek, the water a trickle over black rocks, but it's six feet below me, the other bank just far enough away I can't risk jumping. I have no choice but to follow it, further downhill as the crevice grows wider and wider. Every now and then I peek over the edge, but the rocky sides are too slimy for me to climb down, and then too high. At the snap of a branch behind me I pick up my pace, not worrying about keeping quiet, only about increasing the distance between us. A good idea that doesn't mean jack shit as I come to a cliff.

The creek carries on twenty feet below, widening into a muddy patch of ground before dribbling over the next ridge of rock. Like the banks, the face of the cliff is a sheer drop of crumbling, mossy stone. It's either break my neck trying to show off my nonexistent rock climbing skills, or surrender.

Between the trees, the lake shines silver, the sky a smear of hazy blue. Time slows, each breath feeling like my last, my body forgetting that this is a game, knowing only that I'm caught, and that it's these two men who caught me, as Karl and Wyn converge on me from two directions. Wyn's not even breathing hard, both of them grinning like wolves.

"Well done, little bunny," Karl says, shrugging off his backpack. "That was good fun, if over too soon. Next time I'll give you more of a head start."

He starts to undo his fly, but the game's not over. If I wait any longer I'll lose my last chance, and as they close on me I bolt back the way I came.

Too late, as Karl lunges, grabbing a handful of my sweatshirt and yanking me off my feet. I land hard on my ass, but the sweatshirt fits so loosely that I slither out of it and am up and running again. Straight into Wyn as he throws his arms around me.

Something primal ignites within me and without a thought I sink my teeth into his bicep. He lets me go with a yell, but Karl has caught up and barrels into me, knocking me down again. Does he want to fuck me or kill me? My body can't tell the difference, and scrambling on all fours like the animal I am at heart, I launch myself between them, using the momentum to drive me to my feet.

I've barely taken two strides when an iron bar catches me across the chest. No, it's Carter's arm, which he locks around my throat before I can squirm free.

"For someone who says he doesn't know how to bottom you sure are a brat," he grunts as I batter at him.

"Let me go!" I gurgle as his arm tightens.

"Not a chance, bunny."

I know how to end this. I know what to say to make this stop. There's no fucking way I'm going to call red light, even as the others approach with claws out. Wyn and Karl each grab one of my legs to stop me kicking Carter in the shins, then they hoist me off the ground between them and carry me back to the clearing, where they force me to my knees.

Yes, this, just like I fantasized, even before I met them. Forget Wyn's chatter about no one owning anyone. I want to be owned, be their pet, their toy, the servant of their needs, and as they surround me I get a real sense for how much bigger they are than me. This might actually hurt, but I don't care. Make it hurt, make me doubt myself, make me know myself so I know if this is what I want.

They exchange glances again, a silent negotiation that closes as Wyn and Carter nod and Karl grins. The only one of them who's dick I didn't try to suck. The first one who made me think, *why not? Why can't I have both?*

Now I get all three, a thought so overwhelming that my mind begins to drift, separating from the prison of my body. Carter crouches beside me, putting his arms around me to speak softly in my ear.

"Come back, Reagan. Don't dissociate, baby. Let me know you're in there or we'll have to stop."

"No! I'm fine, I'm here," I pant, blinking to clear my eyes. "Please, don't stop. Not now." Not this close to my dreams coming true.

"I'll be right here," he says, giving me a last squeeze. I nod and he releases me, stepping back as Karl moves closer. The hottest man to ever wear cargo shorts, but I'm going to forgive him as he unzips to reveal a monster. Or does his uncut dick look huge because he's standing over me in broad daylight? I've probably eaten thicker burritos, a thought so absurd I laugh a little as he stops in front of me.

"I'm not laughing at you."

"You had better not be," he says, milking his shaft.

"I'm laughing at me. At what a slut I am." I have to be, the way my dick throbs as I rise on my knees and open my mouth for him.

He swears, some Croatian word that makes Carter chuckle, then steps closer, until his dick is all I see. Setting his hand on my head, he strokes the slippery tip across my lips, letting it drag against my cheeks. He does it again, holding me back subtly as I try to catch him in my mouth.

"Carter is right. You are a brat." Before I can think of a suitably bratty reply, he tips my head back and slides into my mouth. Only the head, but it stretches my lips and jaw wide.

"Come on, brat. Let me in," he murmurs, his fingers playing over my taut cheek. "I heard this was your very favorite thing, to kneel and let a thick cock pry you open."

Sucking air through my nose, I bob my head forward, taking him deeper. Then deeper still, finding a rhythm as he groans encouragement, tilting his hips to give me more. Unsteady on my knees, I grab hold of his thighs, shuffling forward so I don't have to lean, so he can fuck my mouth more easily. I am a slut. And I don't care. For these men, I'll be anything.

His grip tightens in my hair, little pops of sensation shooting down my spine with my every movement, building to a blazing tension in my groin, like someone is sucking me, like I'm sucking myself. If that was a thing, I'd have drowned years ago. This is enough, this is everything—this unthinking obedience, kneeling at their feet, offering myself. This burning ache in my jaw, the ram of his cock against the back of my throat, the growing sense that this is all I've ever done, be a thing that these men fuck, the growing want to never be anything else.

I suck, hollowing my cheeks and making him cry out, more foreign words that have to mean something like *I'm going to come*, because he does, his spunk suddenly filling my mouth.

"Don't swallow that," he growls as he pulls out. Going down on one knee, he grabs my throat. "Open and show me, Reagan. I want to see my come in your pretty mouth."

Of course I do it, even sticking out my tongue a little, not expecting him to shove his fingers deep inside. "So good," he murmurs, smearing his come around inside my mouth, his other hand pinning me in place. "Such a pretty mouth. Like it was made for taking cocks. Does it want another one?"

OURS

CARTER

I'VE NEVER BEEN INTO group scenes. I've certainly never played with or even near my friends. All of us have different tastes, and different groups we move through when looking for a partner. Yet this feels so natural, to be standing here in witness as Karl finger-fucks his own come back into Reagan's mouth. They kiss, moaning into each other, and instead of making me jealous, it only makes me harder.

"Be my guest," Wyn says to me with a little bow.

"No. I want to be last."

"Mmm, sloppy, what, thirds? Carter, you freak."

Grinning, he unbuckles his belt. I know Wyn's more of a show off, that he's played games like this before. Here on this property in fact, and as he runs his fingers through Reagan's hair I promise myself to ask him more about it. After I watch him teach our pet how to deep-throat.

Holding Reagan's head still, he pumps his hips, shoving a little deeper every time. Demanding a little more, Reagan whimpering around Wyn's shaft, digging his nails into his own bare thighs, his eyes rolled to white.

"Come on his face," I blurt, the pressure in my balls intolerable.

"Is that what you like, bunny?" Wyn murmurs. "Taking a faceful of spunk?" Reagan whimpers in the affirmative and Wyn groans, then grabs him by the hair and forces him back on his heels.

"Where the fuck have you been all my life?" he hisses, wrapping his hand around his cock. In a few urgent strokes he's there, his hips pumping as his come spurts across Reagan's face. Reagan cries out in answer, his body jerking like he climaxed as well.

As Wyn staggers to one side I'm ready, pulling Reagan upright by his hair then shoving my aching cock deep into his sticky mouth. He moans softly, then closes his lips around me and starts to suck.

How can he be so good when he's so new? Or was he truly made for this? Made for me, like our meeting was the act of some chaotic god who decided to mix fire and ice. Or was it merely luck that our paths crossed and then recrossed, that this is where we ended up?

I'm ready to start believing in that god as Reagan grabs my hips, pulling himself onto my dick. Asking desperately for me to lose control, pound into him, use his mouth for a fuck-hole.

Who's the slut now? A pointless word, a flail to beat ourselves with, used to shame the nonconforming, and I exile the thought, determined to unpack it later with Reagan. After I've used his mouth as, yes, a fuck-hole.

So would you, if this mouth was yours to use, pink and wet and soft and hard. He's learned a few skills, using his tongue, twisting his head as he bobs up and down, pulling back until only the head is in his mouth, then plunging down on me again. Wyn's come is still smeared across his face, a crop of new freckles sprinkled across his nose from our day in the sun. Kneeling on the dappled forest floor, leaves stuck in his hair, lashes fluttering against his cheeks, he's an enchanted beast given human form, a rare jewel stolen from a dead land. He's mine. He's ours.

My balls tighten, my whole body tensing with the onset of orgasm. I want to make him wait, and myself, to make it that much sweeter, but it's too late, and as the wave breaks I pull him off me then grab my slippery shaft and fuck into my own grip, my come spattering his chin and chest and I don't know what else, my senses overwhelmed, my mind divinely blank.

I come back to my body with a thump. Literally, landing on my naked ass, my hand sticky with come, my lips tingling from the ebbing climax. Wyn is kneeling with Reagan, who lolls with his head on Wyn's shoulder, clutching himself through the wet front of his shorts.

The forest is unchanged, and as I rub my eyes on my reasonably clean shoulder, Karl appears. Squatting beside me he offers me a bottle of water, then Wyn's pack of wipes.

"What a day," he muses as I tuck my dick away. "Though of course it's not even one o'clock."

"I'm starving," I mumble, my tongue as numb as my brain. Karl rummages in his pack then hands me an energy bar.

"Don't be a hero," he says as I push it away. "You've been running around all morning, you just collapsed, and let's be honest, only one of us is as young as he feels."

Even Reagan looks rough, his face stark white, his hands shaking as Wyn helps him to his feet. Karl passes around the rest of the energy bars and we sit on the rocks, eating in silence, soaking in the forest energy, thinking through the implications of what we've done and what we're doing.

"You're quick on your feet," Karl says to Reagan who sits on the ground with his back against a rock. "I thought the terrain would slow you down more."

"I did cross-country for a few years," he replies, his chin on his up-bent knees.. "Mainly to get out of class. But I liked running. It was the only time as a kid I remember feeling...not happy, I guess. More, that I didn't feel anything at all. I wasn't lonely or bored or ashamed or suffocating. I was just a body, moving through space." He notices us gazing at him and blushes. "Sorry. TMI."

"Don't worry about it," Wyn says. "We've all been through some shit."

"But was that okay with everyone?" Reagan asks, slowly sitting upright and unfolding his legs. "I don't mean did I do a good job. You all seemed happy. More, are you happy with each other? Like you aren't all freaked out and hiding it, are you?"

"It's not something we've ever done as friends, but I'd certainly do it again," I say.

He exhales unsteadily. "Sure, but we're not just talking about sex, right? It feels like we're making some kind of commitment. And I don't know how that works when there's more than two people."

"I don't think it's much different," I reply.

"A bit harder to schedule, maybe," Wyn says. "But all healthy relationships depend on communication. On not keeping your fears and your feelings hidden. Even if you're jealous. You don't just react, you work through it together."

"I don't want to hurt anyone," Reagan says softly.

"Of course you don't, but you can't always avoid it," Karl says. "What matters is that you are honest. People can get over hurt feelings. They can't always get over being lied to, even if you did it to protect them."

"I wish...ugh, maybe this sounds stupid, but I wish my parents liked each other," Reagan says, his voice cracking with emotion. "Or at least acted like they did. I don't think I've even seen them hold hands. So yeah, I don't know what normal people do when they fall in love. I was kind of starting to think love wasn't a thing, you know? Like it was just a story people told themselves to justify wanting to fuck someone."

"Have you changed your mind?" I ask.

"I guess? Or I started thinking about love differently. It's not just about who you get together with, it's a thing you feel about people who matter to you. It's like a glue that holds you together. You guys love each other, right?" he asks, looking from one to the other. "But like friends. It doesn't make sense that everyone who ever said they loved their friend secretly wanted to fuck them."

"That's for sure," Karl says with a grin, looking between me and Wyn. "No offense, fellas. I'm sure you'll both make someone very happy one day."

"Bite me, Olaf," Wyn says, laughing as he gets to his feet.

"But you see I would never. You're not my type. And Olaf's a Scandinavian name, you racist."

Wyn laughs even harder, then offers Karl his hand to help him up. They wouldn't be my friends if they couldn't laugh at each other and themselves, as at the last second Wyn whisks his hand away, turns and farts in Karl's face.

Everyone needs a few minutes to get over that one. Even Reagan, both hands clamped over his mouth because his first hoot of laughter scared the birds, tears in his eyes as he rocks back and forth and Karl lies crumpled on the ground like Wyn shot him. My damn friends, and we're still giggling as we carry on along the ridge another hundred meters to the path leading down.

"Are you fucking kidding me?" Reagan blurts, twisting to look behind us. "I was that close to winning?"

"Are you saying that wasn't winning?" Karl says, pointing his thumb at the plateau above.

"Like that wasn't going to happen anyway."

"Maybe you'll do better next time."

Reagan's head whips around. "You'd do that again?"

"Not tomorrow. Although, not *not* tomorrow."

Smirking self-consciously, his cheeks pink, Reagan jogs ahead to catch up with Wyn. Karl and I hang back. We're all going to the same place, and the day is heating up, the cicadas beginning to keen in the treetops. The car is an oven, and despite the AC we're all sweating again by the time we get back to the cottage.

"I need a shower," I groan, wiggling my leg to unstick my ball sack from my thigh.

"Fuck that, I'm going for a swim," Wyn says.

"Good idea," Karl says as Wyn strips off his shirt and starts towards the lake. Damn right it's a good idea, before I cool down and lose my nerve. I don't care what Karl thinks, the cold water is always a shock, but today it's calling to me.

"You coming in?" I say to Reagan, who hasn't moved.

"I might put my feet in or something."

"It's not the warmest but you don't notice after a minute."

He follows me to the shore, where I strip and wade in, trying not to hiss when the water closes over my ankles. Reagan hasn't even taken off his shoes, watching the others mess around with a blankly rigid expression, and I splash back to him.

"What's wrong?"

"I can't swim," he mutters.

"Not at all?"

His eyes fly open. "Shhh. Do you need to tell the whole world?"

"It's okay," I say softly. "You don't have to come in."

"Then they're going to know," he hisses, glancing around me.

I want to tell him that no one cares if he can swim. But there's more going on here. A matter of his pride. His ideas of what a man should and shouldn't do. Ideas I think he'd benefit from giving up, but this isn't the moment to tell him so.

"You don't need to hide anything from us, Reagan. We're all a little fucked up about something, believe me. I'm terrified of spiders."

"Seriously? One hit from a shoe, and boom, no more spider."

"Sure. Unless you're a chickenshit like me who has to get Karl to ID it then kill it then scour the apartment for any survivors while I call my mother."

"Seriously?"

"Not every spider, but yeah. Basically." I clear my throat, keeping my head up so I don't start looking for the little fuckers among the rocks. "So if you've ever wanted to learn to swim, I can help you. I was a lifeguard for a few summers. Lead a few swimming classes. I won't take you deeper than you can touch. But it's up to you. No one is going to think less of you if you don't."

FLOATING

REAGAN

THE WATER LOOKS DELICIOUS, the surface crinkled by the breeze, fading from a soft green brown near the shore to sky blue past where Karl is floating on his back. And maybe Carter's right, and the other men don't care if I don't know how to swim. I care, and I wish I'd done something about it years ago. I can't pass up this chance.

And holy shit, do I ever need to wash. There's so much come in my shorts I didn't even bother dealing with it in the forest, just ignored the slimy sensation, and Carter laughs at the gooey slurp they make as I peel them off.

Then there's nothing between me and the lake but him. He takes my hand and walks with me across the teetering rocks that some asshole probably thinks is a beach and into the icy cold water.

"Fucking fuck!"

"It gets better," he says, chuckling.

"Sure, once my feet go numb." I'm holding his hand too tightly, but like fuck I'm letting go as my feet sink into the silty bottom. "People do this for fun, huh?"

"We can always jump in from the—"

"No the fuck we cannot." I'm stronger than this. It's just water. None of those psychopaths are anywhere near. Not Carter's friends but those so-called friends from that year I went to camp. But I can't think about that, can't stop to process that shitty memory right now as Carter leads me deeper, step by trembling step, until the water is over my knees and the waves that looked so cute from the shore are slapping against my thighs. Carter hasn't said a word except to point out smoother patches of bottom where I don't have to step on the slimy rocks. Everything about this is a fucking joke, proof of why we invented swimming pools, but I'm going to keep trying, damn it. I'm going to break this curse too.

We stop when the water is up to my ass. My balls are vacationing somewhere in my ribcage, and my hand hurts from clutching Carter's, but I'm in the lake, though I don't know how I'm going to make myself go any further.

"How were you in there up to your necks?" I say through my chattering teeth as Wyn and Karl wade towards us.

"You gotta work up to it," Wyn says.

"Or have a nice insulating layer," Karl adds, slapping his belly. "Really, it's nice once you're in."

I glance at Carter, who smiles but doesn't speak. Leaving it up to me if I tell them or not. "I don't know how to swim."

"You never had lessons?" Wyn asked.

"I was already in so many activities. I guess my parents didn't think it was important."

"Well, you have done the hard part and got into the water," Karl says. "We can take you a little deeper if you want."

"Like all of you?"

"If it will help you feel safe."

Safe. I don't even know what that feels like. Don't know what it's like to not be looking over my shoulder, waiting to find out what I did wrong, or wondering who's on my tail trying to knock me out of first place. I can't even speak, but I don't think I need to, as they take up positions around me.

"Ready?" Carter asks, taking my other hand. I nod, even though my heart is pounding and my guts are churning and if I think too much more about any of this I won't be able to do it. Step by step I follow him deeper, until we're past the end of the dock and the water is around my groin, and then my waist. The waves are even stronger here, the water much colder as I cling to his hands.

"Do you want to try floating?" he asks.

"How does that work?" I stammer.

"Humans are pretty buoyant. We'll hold you the whole time." He talks me through the basics, Karl demonstrating beside us. Then it's my turn, and I face the other way so Carter can hold me under my shoulder blades. Karl and Wyn are to either side, waiting to support my hips. It's ridiculous, like some kind of gay séance/baptism, their expressions deadly serious, everyone committed to the bit. I refuse to disappoint them, but I can't keep from whimpering as the cold water touches my ears.

"Remember what I said," Carter murmurs, his forearms bracing the back of my head. "You can still touch the bottom here. Keep your butt up and breathe."

And then I'm floating and…it's nice. Nothing life-changing, except for the fact that I'm doing it at all. Thinking this is enough to break the spell as my ass starts to sink. Immediately I feel their hands buoying me up, Carter murmuring his instructions to keep breathing, stay calm, trust him. I do, like I've never trusted anyone. All of them, these men I've only known a few weeks, who have shown me more kindness and honesty than anyone in my life.

"Are you okay?" Carter says, sinking low to speak to me.

"Yeah," I rasp, emotion clogging my throat. "Thanks."

"Stretch out your arms, it'll help you stay up."

I do, fanning my fingers and letting my legs drift apart. I can't feel Wyn and Karl's hands, only Carter's, rock steady beneath my shoulder blades as he gazes down at me with a sweet little smile. Beyond him is the sky, perfectly blue except for one half formed cloud that soon drifts out of sight.

"How are you doing?" Carter asks.

"Hmm…"

"Good to hear."

"Do we have to stop?"

"Not yet." Karl wades up and whispers in his ear and he laughs softly. "You guys are filthy."

"What do they want?" I ask him.

"Only to make you the happiest you've ever been," Karl says, drifting back to my side. "Just relax and keep breathing. Baldwin, a little help, if you don't mind?"

Carter sinks down in the water again, his hands sliding farther down my back until my head rests on his shoulder. Wyn lowers himself as well, one arm under my ass, the other beneath my knees, not holding me up but simply present. A safety net so I know I'm not going to go under as Karl bends over me to enclose my sad, shrunken dick in his hot mouth.

"Keep breathing, Reagan," Carter murmurs as my body stiffens in shock. Not that it hurts. If anything it's too good, as the hungry sucking of Karl's supple tongue and lips coax me back to life. When I'm as hard as I've ever been, he stops, letting my dick slap wetly against my stomach, my protest dying as he takes me in his hand.

"You are so delicious," he hums as he starts to work my slick shaft. "I stopped because I know how much you love getting rained on by come. I wondered if it worked as well when it's your own."

I hope to fuck he doesn't need me to answer. I hope this never ends, this weightless, trembling joy. His strokes make my body bob in the water, but Carter and Wyn won't let me go. They want this too, want me to be happy, want me. My drifting hands meet Karl's slippery body on one side and Wyn's on the other. Carter's breath flows over my wet chest, the sky and the water and everything melding together in one epic eruption of shivering pleasure, my body seeming to levitate as my come spatters on my stomach and the water.

"God. Damn," Wyn breathes. "You were right, man. That was hot as fuck."

"You two planned this?" Carter asks as Karl splashes a few handfuls of cool water over me.

"Not planned," Karl says, winking at me. "But not *not* planned."

Wyn lets go of my back end and I let my feet drop. Except the bottom is a lot further down than I expected, the water up around my armpits, making me grab for Carter's arms. Together we wade out of the lake, where I discover that my legs have been replaced with cheese strings.

"Holy fuck," I groan, leaning on him as I drag my feet across the grass. "Did I leave my spine in the lake?"

"Only a little of it," Karl says as he passes. He returns from the cottage with an armful of towels and the two of them bundle me up like a burrito. So well that I can hardly move my legs. Or my arms, the way Karl tucked the third towel around my shoulders.

"Um, guys...a little help?"

Karl and Carter share a look across me. They nod at each other, then bend their legs and hoist me shrieking off the ground. "This isn't what I meant," I holler as they trundle me towards the cottage.

"Pish-posh, whatever gets the job done," Karl says, though I'm happy to hear the strain in his voice. I expect them to set me down at the bottom of the stairs to the deck, but instead they run me right around to the front door.

"Special delivery," Karl calls, tipping an imaginary hat.

"I'll take it from here," Carter chuckles. He opens the door for me and I waddle to my bedroom, where I peel off the towels then flop naked onto the bed. The quiet is immense after spending all day surrounded by the sounds of wind and water, the rustle of leaves. Except it's only two in the afternoon. Plenty of day left to do something else for the first time.

I hope Carter asks why I was afraid of the water, so I can get it off my chest. I hope he never asks, so I never have to think about it again. Maybe it's something else best saved for Dr. Whitman. What matters right now is that I dared to do something despite my fears, that I didn't let my trauma inform my decision making. A month ago I would have roasted anyone who tried to use that sort of language. Now it feels natural to look back on my childhood as the unhappy time it was. To admit that even if my parents had good intentions, the outcome was trash: a moody, insecure, bitter little con artist of a son who had to lose everything he valued to learn that none of it was worth a damn.

And now I'm a slutty, cock-sucking gay boy who lets three men use him like a Fleshlight and has an orgasm whenever someone comes on his face. And I'm happy. Finally, I'm happy.

THE PET

KARL

WYN WON'T LET US cook for him and I cooked last night, so while Carter starts making lunch, or dinner seeing as it's nearly three o'clock, I settle on the couch with the book I keep trying to read. I get through the standard three paragraphs before Reagan sidles out of his room, dressed for the first time in days in something other than my old sweatshirt.

"Laundry's too much to ask for, right?" he asks as he sits cautiously on the other end of the couch.

"Sad to say. Do you need another sweatshirt?"

"Maybe later if we go outside."

"That may not happen this evening," I say, nodding to the bank of lumpy clouds marching across the horizon. As he fidgets I set aside my book once more then beckon him nearer. He glances towards the kitchen then slides across the couch about five centimeters.

"Come here, zečić." I reach for him. He gets the message and scoots nearer, tucking his legs up as I wrap my arm around him. Little by little, he relaxes, until he's nuzzling into my shoulder, his hand on my thigh, his breathing so slow I start to wonder if he's sleeping.

"Hmm...you're cuddly," he murmurs, his hair brushing my beard.

"Thank you. That's a compliment, right?"

"Of course. Why wouldn't it be? I love your tummy."

"Good, because it's not going anywhere. Believe me, I've tried."

"Don't ask me for any hacks."

"Of course not. This is it. This is me." I slap the side of my belly that he's not attached to like a barnacle.

"Will you tell me something?" he asks as he begins to trace a tickling circle round my navel.

"Anything."

"How do you say 'daddy' in Croatian?"

For a moment I can't react, as the blood drains from my brain and fills my cock in a dizzying titration. I've never desired another person so strongly, and we've already fucked twice today. "Are you trying to flatter me, zečić?"

"Maybe. Do you want me to?"

Only if you'd like me to crave you every night and day, dedicate my life to your worship, destroy all who would oppose you. "Very much so."

"So what is it?"

"Tata."

"Tata?" he repeats, and though he doesn't have the correct inflection I shiver. I may have created a monster.

"I like it," I say as he settles against me again.

"Me too." He lets his hand drift downward until it closes over the rigid outline of my cock. "You really like it, don't you, Tata?" he purrs, stroking me through my clothes, which suddenly feel much too small.

"Maybe it's you."

"Maybe it's both."

"An alchemical union."

He frowns briefly. "Sure. Whatever you want."

"What I want is to kiss you while you do that," I say.

"Can I suck you off?"

"Unbelievable. I didn't say no," I add as he pulls his hand away. "I have never known a man with such a singular fixation."

"It's called a fetish, dude."

"Fetish, fixation, po-tay-to, po-tah-to, let's not quibble when you could be getting on your knees."

He scrambles off the couch like I've offered him a prize for good behavior. I am the prize, his eyes rolling closed in ecstasy as he sucks the drop of precome from the reddened tip. At last he can take his time, and he does, bathing my shaft and my balls with his tongue until my fingernails are gouging holes in the upholstery and his spit is running down my crack. I want his mouth everywhere on me, want to make this last even longer, but there's something inhibiting about getting blown on the couch while your friends make dinner a few meters away.

But also thrilling. He wants them to see him like this, see how needy he is, how shameless. He keeps me here, poised between the joy and the cringe, half wondering if I should stop him, but before I act he tightens his grip around the base of my cock and starts to suck.

Phenomenal. I've paid for worse head, and I quit trying to hold back my groans of pleasure as he takes me deep into his throat. Much more and I'm done for, and I tap him clumsily on the head. "If you don't want to swallow this, stop."

He doesn't stop. He wants me to come in his mouth. He wants me to come, so I do, my back arching, hips rising off the upholstery as I unload. He takes it all, his body rocking with mine, his other hand inside his track pants so that he follows me over the edge while I'm still in his mouth. Alchemy indeed, and he the catalyst, transforming sexual energy into this drowsy dreamy state of perfect comfort, aftershocks of orgasm sparking through my limbs, Reagan's insatiable mouth still nursing on my semi-hard on. I'm tempted to let him keep at it, give the poor little thing what he so obviously wants, when Carter looms over me from behind the couch.

"I see the two of you already had dessert," he says. Reagan flinches but doesn't stop, looking up at Carter from between my feet.

"Don't worry, there's plenty for all," I say. "Isn't that right, zečić?"

Bless him, he nods. Stepping back, Carter laughs. "There's actual food if you want it," he says returning to the kitchen. "And no, it's not sausages."

It's pulled chicken burritos (with jackfruit for Wyn), which makes Reagan crack up for some reason he's laughing too hard to be able to explain to the rest of us. I can only imagine. The guy is half eel, the way he unhinges his jaw. A nasty joke I immediately store in the vault of Wrong Things, a wicked little corner of my psyche that no one else has ever seen nor ever will. Don't pretend that you aren't the same, but what makes or breaks our society is whether we are wise enough to keep that chamber closed to everyone but ourselves. Own your demons, but don't let them become other people's problem.

As I expected, the evening turns to rain, a steady drumming that dampens the air and makes everyone agree when I suggest using the fireplace. Which Carter immediately commandeers, because he is a closeted arsonist. Another one for the vault; I am, after all, a very good person.

Other than the distant star of the range hood, the only light comes from the fire, a fluid, ruddy glow that reminds me how far we are from the city. Reagan's sitting sideways on the couch, his back against the arm and his perennially bare legs draped across my lap, for he had to change out of those track pants. Though there's plenty of liquor no one seems inclined to drink. It has been a long day, and I can't be the only one who's happy to stay clear-headed, as our conversation drifts to gender identity and at last polyamory.

Because that is what this is. Not something that I have ever considered doing except in the general sense, accepting it on a philosophical level but never expecting I would be lucky enough to find even one lover, never mind...but no. I still have only one lover. Who wants to be shared.

And yet it feels like enough. I had already made peace with my bachelor's life, even though being bisexual ought to double my dating pool. I can only be myself—hairy, chubby, nose in a book, mind in the gutter—and somehow this bright young thing wants me. Craves me. A passion so strong I'd fear to be its sole target. Reagan has set my tiny world ablaze, and I'm ready to let it burn.

"I feel better knowing that we're all virgins at this," he says, the firelight painting him in gleaming gold and secret red. "That'd be kind of fucked, if you guys went around adopting random freaks all the time."

"Do you think you're a freak?" I ask him.

"I don't know. Maybe. I guess not, if I think about it. There's plenty of videos I've noped out of cause I didn't realize where they were going until they, you know, went there."

"I'm curious what it is you like so much about giving head," Wyn asks him. "Having your mouth full of cock? Feeling it deep in your throat? Or when that come hits your face."

Reagan shivers, digging his heels into the armrest beside me. "All of it, but yeah, that last part. I really don't know why. Even before I came out, you could peep the search history and it's pretty obvious."

"You don't need to be embarrassed," Carter says. "Everyone likes different things."

"But what if that's all I like? Aren't you ever going to want to fuck me?"

"Baby, we are fucking," Wyn says with a chuckle, his teeth catching the golden light.

"Um, not really."

"Yeah, really. You seriously going to tell me that what we did in the forest, what we did in the lake is foreplay?"

He wrinkles his nose. "I guess not."

"You can relax and let go of this heteronormative shit. You don't need to spread your legs for anyone."

Reagan shivers again, pulling down the hem of the sweater I loaned him, though it's not as bulky as my sweatshirt and can't conceal his stiffening cock. "But what if I wanted to?"

"Then we'll take it slow," Wyn replies. "If you don't like something, we stop doing it. Even if you thought you wanted it. Consent isn't a tick box, it's an active engagement with your sexual partner. It's the heart of intimacy. You can't count on your partner to read your signals."

"And no one here is going to judge you if you tap out," Carter adds. "You're safe here, Reagan."

"Safe," he echoes bitterly, his gaze drifting to the fire. "I wouldn't know what that felt like if it fucked me in the mouth."

I want to gather him into my arms, but he's not a child, he's a grown man. Yet when I take his hand he uses it to lever himself onto my lap, not crying, simply shaking as I wrap my arms around him.

"I'm such a mess."

"Shh. You're safe."

Again the word makes him flinch, as if it means the opposite. I'm going to tear the heart out of whoever hurt him this deeply. Wyn joins us on the couch and sets his hand on the back of Reagan's neck to ground him. Gradually our breath synchronizes—Baldwin and Reagan and myself inhaling and exhaling in meditative harmony. We're going to heal this broken boy. We're going to give him back his life.

BOUNDARIES

REAGAN

EXHAUSTED BY MY MELTDOWN, I don't argue when Karl orders me to go to bed, where I drift to sleep on the low hum of their voices. The next morning I wake up even earlier than the day before, but not so early that Wyn and Karl aren't already in the kitchen. I stay out of their way, curled up in a chair by the picture window, nursing a sweet coffee.

Fog covers the lake, Carter visible as a hazy black ghost at the end of the dock, but before I get motivated to go out and join him he starts back towards the house. Right on time for our breakfast of amazingly good vegan pancakes, though the pound of bacon Karl cooked doesn't hurt.

I make sure to offer to do the dishes. Wyn helps, which I don't argue about because he knows where all the stuff goes in the kitchen. Plus it's nice to have help, to know that everyone's working together and not taking turns serving each other. I'm the only one serving, but being their bottom doesn't make me their slave. It just means I love dick.

"What's so funny?" Wyn asks, taking another glass from the drying rack.

"I can't figure out why I'm so happy."

"Why wouldn't you be?"

"I've been letting three guys use my throat as a sperm bank. I'm still broke, still unemployed, still homele—I mean unhoused. Still a subby little slut who doesn't know his limits."

"In other words, about as messed up as everyone else. No one has their shit together. You know that, right?"

"That's not what it looks like."

"No shit. Most people don't go around baring their scars. But we're all only a few bad days away from going through the same thing as you. Maybe less getting used as a sperm bank," he adds with a laugh, "but don't assume that having a high sex drive means that you don't have boundaries. You must, because you were worried earlier about not liking anal."

"Just because I've never done it," I say as he grabs a handful of cutlery.

"That's a boundary too. You can move the line any time you like."

"Is that an invitation?"

"Not unless you want it to be. I'm not fucking with you, honest," he says, still smiling. "You and me in the arbor? That was one of the hottest things I've ever done in my life."

"Seriously? I didn't even touch you."

"I know. So don't worry that I need to get up you to want to be with you." As I drain the sink he closes the drawer and hangs the dishcloth on its rail, always so polite. Or not, as he moves up behind and sets his hands on my hips.

"Maybe we'll try it again sometime," he says, his velvet voice making me shiver as I rinse the suds off my hands.

"Anytime you want. You don't even have to ask."

"You mean, all I have to do is tell you to shove your fingers in your pretty mouth and you'll do it?"

Of course I do. Anything he asks, I'll do. Even let him fuck my ass, if he asks really nice. I think, but I'm going to trust him. Trust that he wasn't lying. That what I give him is enough. It must be enough, as he groans, his hard-on wedging itself between my ass cheeks.

"Bunny, you are something else," he murmurs, slipping his arm around my waist while his other hand palms my dick through my shorts. "Show me how hard you are."

He steps back so I can turn around, licking his lips as I yank my shorts down and claw my sweater out of the way. Just in time for Carter to saunter out of his bedroom.

"Ah, I see we're having come-slut for lunch," he says, his smile growing as he looks me over. And his dick, distending the front of his track pants as behind him Karl comes whistling out of the bathroom wearing nothing but a towel.

"It's a bit early for that, isn't it?" he says as he joins us.

"He started it," I say, pointing at Wyn with my chin.

"And will he finish it or will he leave us all in suspense?"

"You want to watch me work him?" Wyn says, rubbing his cock through his clothes.

"You know I do."

"Let's ditch the kitchen. This might take a while."

I leave my shorts where they fell and follow them to the seating by the fireplace. I'm tempted to leave Karl's sweater on, the air still damply cool from the morning's fog, but Carter gets the fire blazing in record time, while the others move the coffee table out of the way and I stand there looking cute or some shit. If they wanted my help, they'd ask. Maybe they think I'll have enough to do.

Wyn sits on the couch and slaps his thighs. He wants me there, propped up in front of everyone. On display for their pleasure, and as a thousand horny reels start spooling through my brain I sit my naked ass down on Wyn's lap. I'm going to trust him, trust all of them, to tell me what to do. Trust them to stop if I ask. Trust them to still care about me once they're done using me.

His arm across my chest, Wyn settles back into the cushions, making me recline, my legs splayed over his, my dick lying against my belly. "Mmm-mm, you are a sweet little thing," he purrs in my ear, running a hard hand down my body. "Show them how pretty you are when you stroke yourself."

As I wrap my hand around my rock hard dick he guides my other hand to my mouth. The full show, but if that's what he wants, I'm going to give it everything, follow his instructions to the letter.

"Wait," Carter cries as I start to pump my arm. He jumps up and dashes to the bathroom and comes back with an armful of beach towels

"I want that five hundred dollar deposit back," he says as he lays them over the rug at Wyn's feet and the couch to either side of us. "Iain knows what jizz stains look like."

"So you can go hard, bunny," Wyn purrs as I start stroking. "Make a mess of yourself. Don't hold back."

As if I could. As if I want to. Even though this is the most humiliating sex I've ever had, splayed out naked, sucking at my fingers in rhythm with the pumping of my other hand, jerking off for these men like they're paying me.

Wyn is biting at my neck, his hands holding my thighs apart, his bricked out dick digging a hole in my back. The others stand over me, Carter holding his waistband down while he strokes himself with his other hand, Karl naked from the shower, pinching his nipples, his hips rocking in time with mine. If this is being a slut then bring it on because I've never felt so wanted, so fucking centered in my own life. So significant and irreplaceable, because all these men want me.

No matter how perfect my life has seemed, how unbearably privileged, what good is privilege if it becomes a wall between you and the world? I want to be in the world, the ragged, stinking, horny world, full of real, stinking, horny people. I want the kind of love that can't be bought, the kind that only comes if you give it in return. I want to live.

If I live, as Wyn's firm grip closes around my wrist. "I said stop, bunny."

"You're a cruel top, Baldwin," Carter rasps.

"Just for that, you can stop too. And you too, Veselko."

"You fucker," Karl growls.

"Tell me it won't be so much better if you wait. And you," he says, speaking softly to me alone. "Are you ready to serve us with that mouth?"

I nod, my tongue lolling, my brain liquefied. All I know is how to let them fuck me, as Wyn sits me up on his knees, holding my wrists together behind my back. Carter beats Karl in rock-paper-scissors for the right to go first, setting his hand on my head to angle my mouth.

"How the hell did I get so lucky?" he murmurs, painting my open lips with the head of his dick. "Two minutes either way and I'd have never found you."

I don't know what he's trying to say. I don't know anything except this need to have that thickness pry me open, sanctify my unholy mouth. Make me who I was meant to be.

Because it's so fucking good, his dick. So good to taste as he slides against my tongue, to smell as I furrow into his thick pubes. Even the pain's delicious, as he shoves against the back of my throat, my jaw stretched wide around his solid girth, my thighs trembling as I can't quite touch the floor.

On Baldwin's order Karl steps in, though this tummy means I can't get as much of his dick as I want. It must not be working for him either as he taps my head to stop me then goes to whisper in Wyn's ear.

"Mmm, nice. How about it, bunny? Ever wonder what it's like to get eaten by a bear?"

"No, but let's fucking go," I slur, though I'm not even sure what I've agreed to as Karl lies down on the rug.

"Lie on a towel or I'm making you steam clean the rug," Carter says tersely.

Grumbling, Karl spreads the towel over the carpet then lies down again. "Now come here, bunny, and mount that virgin ass of yours on my face."

Wyn lets me go and I slither off his lap, falling over myself in my hurry to straddle Karl. He poses me facing his feet, then spreads my ass cheeks and sighs. "You are so utterly gorgeous."

I don't know what to say, couldn't speak either way as he exhales over my sensitive skin, a sensation like nothing I know. That's not a part of my body I touch unless absolutely necessary, despite all the times I've jacked off to a guy getting his ass blown out. This feels necessary, like an insight during therapy, a moment of understanding what it is I really want from life.

I relax, letting myself sink down until his hands are supporting me. A little lower and I feel the first soft trace of his tongue, not against my hole but trailing up one side of my crack then down the other. He keeps this up, taunting me, making me want it more and more with every graze of his tongue against my rim. I can't think past the feeling, the hot, slick, tickling, taunting, irreplaceable sensation, and I laugh out loud to think that I've denied myself this and believed that's what made me a man.

I am a man no matter what. I am a man who loves to get his ass eaten by a gorgeous, goofy bear with a sexy tummy and a beard that tickles my thighs as I ride his face. I am myself no matter what, and this is who I am.

A man who shivers with raw anticipation at the sight of Wyn dropping his pajama pants. Because it's ten in the morning and all the four of us have achieved so far today is to eat pancakes and fuck me. More, more, and then maybe more pancakes, but right now what matters is

Wyn's beautiful dick and Wyn's beautiful hand around that dick and the question of whether I can get that dick in my mouth.

"Tata," I whimper, hoping Karl can hear me. His tongue stills. "Please can I suck Wyn's dick?" He flashes a thumbs up then goes back to rimming me.

Licking his lips, Wyn stands astride him, milking himself even harder. Teasing me, because Karl's hands are locked on my hips, keeping me mounted on his unstoppable tongue, keeping me from reaching Wyn's dick.

Wyn knows what I want, laughing as he sets his hand on my head, holding me back as he inches nearer and I whimper in frustration.

"Easy, bunny," he coos. "We've got all day for this."

"I can't wait," I gasp. "Please, Wyn."

"Is our little bunny going to pop off?" he says, threading his fingers through my hair.

"I wanna come while you're fucking me."

"Where do you want me to nut? In your mouth? Or in your face."

"Mouth."

"Good boy, answering so quickly. Now let's give you what you want. A nice fat dick down your throat."

He makes me work, lick him all over, suck at his balls, everything except the thing I want the most. My ass is a quivering, sloppy mess, Karl's tongue actively fucking my hole, Wyn's hand on my head pinning me down. At last he pushes into my panting mouth. Deeper, bumping his hips to shove in little by little, until my jaw aches from stretching around his shaft and his thick head fills my throat and I'm a breathless, helpless, writhing thing between two points of limitless pleasure, beyond my body yet totally rooted in it, feeling every sensation, impossibly alive.

And then I die. Figuratively, but that's what the French sometimes call orgasm, the little death, as a hand wraps around my leaking dick. Carter's, I understand later, but in this moment it's a disembodied touch that sends me spiraling into an earth-shattering climax, cold fire racing through my veins as my balls turn inside out, my come spurting over Karl's furry chest. I'm still vibrating when Wyn groans from the depths of his soul, grabbing my hair and thrusting deep as his come fills my mouth.

It's everything I wanted, everything I feared. The life I was meant to live, and all I had to do was give up everything.

PARENTAL AUTHORITY

CARTER

AFTER OUR OUTRAGEOUS MORNING, we take it easy for the rest of the day, reading or working on the jigsaw puzzle, Reagan bouncing between us, cuddling up on the couch or perching on the kitchen counter while I make a snack. Mid-afternoon, we take him swimming again and he floats on his own for the first time. It's a lazy summer Wednesday at the cottage and as I sit on the end of the dock chair with a can of IPA in one hand and Reagan's hand in the other, I feel a tension in me begin to unwind. Like I've been holding my breath all my life and can finally let it out.

"Thank you," Reagan says out of nowhere.

"For what?" I chuckle.

"For everything. I still don't know what made you take a chance on me."

"Neither do I. Sometimes I get burned when I do that, trust my gut. This time I got lucky. We all did."

"You saved my life."

"Not really."

"Maybe. I don't know what I would have done. How I would have gone on living."

"Could you not have called your parents? If it was either them or a shelter bed?"

He shivers despite the sun, his gaze far away. "Maybe. But I didn't have to, so it doesn't matter."

"Do they even know you lost your job?"

"I haven't talked to them since Easter."

"Dude..."

"Don't even bother," he says, jerking his hand from mine. "You have no fucking idea." He heaves himself out of the low chair and stalks towards the house with his head between his shoulders, blowing past Karl who's stopped to talk to him, and nearly jerking the patio door off the rail.

"What did you say?" Karl asks when I meet him at the head of the dock.

"I asked about his parents."

"Oh, don't do that," Karl says, his eyes widening.

"I didn't know it would trigger him like that. He never talks about them."

"He's told me many things. His father should be careful if he meets me. I have some questions he will not enjoy answering."

"Don't make it harder for Reagan. They already don't get along."

"I'm not going to fight him," he says, walking with me back to the house. "I'm just going to yell at him. A lot. Hopefully in front of witnesses."

I expect Reagan to be in his room, but as soon as I step inside he's on me, clinging to my neck, breathing hard through his nose like he does when he's trying not to cry.

"I didn't mean it," he blurts as I stroke his back. "I'm not mad at you. I'm sorry."

"It's okay. I didn't realize it was this bad."

"Neither did I, really. Not until I met you. Until I saw how wrong they were. So I can't go back there. Not now. He won't put up with me now."

"Now that you're woke?"

He laughs bitterly and then it's too much for him and he breaks down in hacking sobs. Broken, but on the mend. Broken, but still a whole person. All he needs is time to heal.

He stays attached to my side for the rest of the day, while we eat charcuterie and finish the jigsaw puzzle, then sit out by the fire until the pile of wood is gone. He says very little, but he's smiling, and that's enough. Following me to bed, he snuggles close, his head burrowed in the hollow of my shoulder, his smoky hair tickling my chin. I've never been so needed and it's starting to scare me, but I won't bug him with my fears when he can barely manage his own. One of us has to be strong.

Yet again I'm the last to wake up the next morning. Reagan is helping Karl make sandwiches for what looks like a long hike, and as I help myself to coffee his phone rings on the island. He picks it up to check the number then immediately flicks the call away and puts down his phone again.

"A scammer?" I ask.

"My dad," he replies. "Karl, weren't you going to put pickles in these?"

Karl slaps himself in the forehead. "You're right, they're nothing without the pickles." As he opens the fridge, Reagan's phone rings, and he again checks the number then sends the call to voicemail.

"Doesn't he take a hint?"

Neither of them reply so I take my own advice and go out to the deck, where Wyn is in the middle of a yoga pose.

"Motherfucker's been calling all morning," he mutters as the sound of Reagan's phone filters through the patio door.

"He should put it on mute. No, he should block him."

"He can't block his father. What if there's an emergency?"

Leaving him to his warrior pose, I wander back inside. Reagan is curled up on the couch, scrolling his phone, and glances up at me. "I don't want to talk to him. He's just going to yell at me, and I'm done with his shit."

"You sure it's not something important?"

"No, because then my mom would—ah fuck."

"Is that her?"

He shoots me a finger gun. As he gets up my phone rings. No one should be calling me, but when I see my landlord's number I answer.

"Hey, Gurdeep, what's up?"

"You tell me. There is a madman on my porch saying you have stolen his son."

"Excuse me?"

"Reagan, the boy's name is."

"Reagan's with me, but he's an adult."

"Really? I thought he was twelve or thirteen from the way this man speaks. Oh well, I will tell his father he's alive. And you tell this Reagan to answer his damn phone. The madman has been here all morning and I can't get him to go away."

"I was actually going to ask you about putting Reagan on the lease when I got back from the cottage."

"Why, is he living with you?"

"He lost his apartment. We thought it would only be a couple days but you know what vacancies are like."

"That's very well, but please can you come and do something about his father? I'm sorry to bother you while you're away, but if he won't leave I will have to call the cops. And it'd be my luck they'll arrest me. This man looks like money. White money."

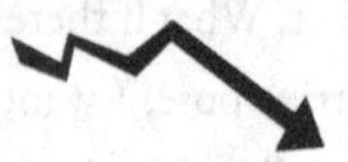

Wyn insists on coming, as the truck's in his name. Following Karl's zig-zagging navigation, he avoids the small towns along the way and we don't hit traffic until we're at Highway 400.

I call Gurdeep when we're a few minutes away, but he doesn't answer. We've been on the road for three hours and my knees ache from being bent. Reagan's slumped against the door, chewing on his sleeves and looking sick, and I resolve to protect him in any way I can. No one deserves to grow up without love, and it would go a long way to explain why he is the way he is, so desperate for approval, so weighed down by shame.

Gurdeep calls me back as Wyn is parking the truck. "I'm here, we're just parking."

"Good, good. He got back in his car but he hasn't left. Oh and he is getting out now."

Across the street, a middle aged blond man is getting out of a smoked out BMW parked in front of a fire hydrant. An even blonder woman the same age gets out too.

"Shit," Reagan hisses, ducking behind the truck. "I'm so not ready to deal with him."

"Don't worry. We're not going to let this get out of hand."

"How the fuck did he even find me?" He's trembling, his pupils blown out, his whole body poised to run. My hands are aching and I relax my balled fists, pushing aside my sincere wish to shove them into the blond man's face.

"Where is this father of yours?" Karl growls as he joins us on the sidewalk, his nostrils flaring like a bull. I love him, but he's no good in fights.

"Please don't start any shit," I tell him. "This is going to be enough of a pain in the ass without you escalating."

"He's who escalated—"

"Don't. Don't even start. Remember Kingston?"

He deflates a little, his face heating. "Yes. I remember Kingston. Point taken."

"Being present will be enough of a help. In case things get out of hand."

"Aye, captain."

By now Wyn has joined us and we start for the house, where Gurdeep is on the front steps arguing with Reagan's dad. A broader, taller version of his son, with paler eyes and the attenuated skin of a plastic surgery addict, he's wearing tight blue golf pants and an aggressively orange polo shirt in what can only be described as a high fashion take on a utility worker's high visibility gear. Reagan's mother looks almost but not exactly like a Barbie doll, her white blouse dotted with little oranges that suggest she dressed to match her mate, or maybe the other way around, as there's apparently a world of adult men who don't know how to dress themselves.

At last they notice us, as Reagan's mother gasps and comes teetering towards him on her blue Jimmy Choos.

"Honey, what's happened?" she coos, patting his arm. "Where are your clothes?"

"I sold them," he replies bluntly. "Why is he here?"

"We were so worried about you."

"The fuck you were."

Her face goes white beneath her foundation. "We really were. Thankfully your old landlord gave us your address, otherwise we would have had to call the police."

"The police? Why?"

"To file a missing person's report."

"Seriously? The first time in your life you give a shit about me and it's because I won't return your calls? Have you ever considered that I meant it when I told you that I hate you?" he says to his dad.

"Reagan, he's your father," his mother warns. "You can't hate him."

"Wanna bet?"

"You better start explaining what happened, young man," his dad says, planting his fists on his hips.

"I got fired," Reagan replies in that same blank tone. "I stole from the company and Ajay fired me. Then I couldn't make my condo payments. And now I'm living here."

"With them?" he sneers, jerking his head towards us.

"I didn't have a lot of options."

"Don't you have friends who could help you?" his mother asks, her false lashes fluttering.

"Not since Mitch screwed me over. Oh right, that's the other reason I'm unhoused, because fucking Mitch locked me out of my crypto wallet and wiped me out."

Reagan's dad frowns, "Why would he do that?

"Duh, to rip me off. Hello?"

"Why didn't you try harder to keep your job?"

"How would that have worked? Are you even listening? I stole like fifteen thousand dollars. I should be in jail right now."

"And you didn't think to ask Mitch what happened to the money?"

Groaning, Reagan rolls his eyes. "How am I gonna ask him? I can't even find him."

"And you didn't talk to the police?" his mom asks, almost but not quite touching her husband's arm, though I don't know which of these textbook Tories needs comforting the most.

"What am I going to say to them?" Reagan replies. "Hey guys, can you help me recover money someone stole from me that I stole from someone else first?"

"And you're sure it was Mitch?" his dad asks.

"There's no one else it could have been."

"What a shame," his mother says. "He was such a nice young man."

"He's a con artist. So was I, if we're being honest."

His father sucks in a whistling breath through his cosmetically corrected nose. "You mean to say you lost your job, your condo, and all your friends, and now you're crying poor to me?"

"Excuse me, but when did that happen? I didn't ask you for shit. Why would I ever expect you to do anything for me?"

"How dare you?" his father grates through his capped teeth, red blotches rising across his face. "After all we've done for you."

"Everything you did *to* me," Reagan retorts. "You never cared whether I liked all those activities you signed me up for. Never once asked how I felt. It was all for my future, my fantastic fucking future. That future's a dumpster fire and I've been an asshole for most of my life, so good work, really great parenting." As he starts applauding sarcastically his father turns to me and looks me in the eye for the first time.

"I suppose you people think this is hilarious, a father fighting to save his son."

"Not at all, sir," I reply with much more calm than I feel. "Reagan's been really struggling to get back on his feet."

"And I'm meant to bail him out, am I?"

"That's probably what I'd do. He is your son, after all."

"He's a failure."

Reagan and his mother have been talking softly to one side but at this he spins on his heel. "You know what, Dad? Fuck you. I'm fucking done. Don't call me, don't text me, don't ever fucking speak to me again, you piece of shit sorry ass excuse for a father."

"Unbelievable," his father says as Reagan stomps up the front steps, his shoulders hunched around his ears. "Eighty-five thousand dollars—"

Reagan whirls around, incandescent. "Oh my god, shut up about that!" he shouts. "I didn't make you spend that money. I didn't ask to go to private school. I begged you to let me go to regular school, with normal kids. I don't care how much you spent, because I didn't make that choice."

"You're lucky we did."

"Am I? Because what did it get me? Therapy, and disaster. I didn't learn a thing about living. Not a goddamn thing about how to treat other people like they matter, how to look past the end of my own nose and think about why someone's suffering. How to sit with my discomfort until I figure out what's really triggering it, what part of myself is lashing out in fear."

"Honey, what are you talking about?" his mother says, fluttering her mink lashes.

He clutches his hair with a strangled shriek of frustration. "I went woke, alright? I'm fucking woke." Spitting with fury, he ticks off his credentials with his fingers. "I'm gay, and I'm polyamorous, and one of my metamours is Black, and fuck the system, and fuck the banks and the police, and Pride was a fucking riot."

He stands panting as his parents gape at him. Everywhere around us, normal life goes on. A skateboarder dekes around Karl, who waits on the sidewalk with a guard-dog's waning patience. A squirrel watches the human drama from atop a neighbor's fence. Everything is ordinary, even this fight, as yet another jackass realizes that the child he raised to be his mirror has a life of his own.

"Go away," Reagan says tiredly as his dad draws breath. "Just go. Whatever you're going to say, I don't want to hear it. Tell me in an email."

"You come back here this instant, young man," Reagan's father shouts as his son goes to step through the door. He turns to his father with a wobbly smile.

"I don't have to do what you tell me. Not anymore." As he enters his house his father rounds on us with a sneer.

"I see how it is. You dirty groomers think you can just—"

With an open shout Reagan comes thumping down the stairs, stopping just inside the door. "You shut your goddamn mouth," he snarls, stabbing his finger at his father. "I'm twenty fucking six, you dumb fuck. No one's getting groomed. Except you, by your bullshit beliefs, and the assholes in the media who enable them."

"Reagan, honey," his mother says, but he retreats further into the house. When his father moves to follow, I step in front of him.

"Get the fuck out of my way," he spits, trying to dodge around me.

"Your son doesn't want to talk to you right now."

"This is none of your goddamn business."

"Sir, I think you should get back in your car."

His eyes swell, his eyebrow quivering. "Look, you fucking fa—"

"Are you really going to finish that word?" Wyn snaps as I stand up to my full height, letting him see what he's up against. I hate taking advantage of my size, but this piece of shit needs to learn some humility.

"I'm going to need you to get in your car and go away," I say. Calmly, evenly, conscious of my hammering heart, the slick of saliva that fills my mouth as my adrenaline spikes.

"Let's go, Brett," his wife murmurs. She tentatively touches his arm and he whirls about, nearly elbowing her in the face.

"Easy does it," I say, stepping forward with my hands raised.

"You stay the hell away from me!" he snarls, spinning back around with his fist cocked.

"Brother, you better not start swinging," Wyn says, but Reagan's dad ignores him, waving his fists at me like he's seen too many MMA pay-per-views.

"Give me back my son," he snarls at me.

"Your adult son?" I say, lowering my hands now that we're past the stage of de-escalation and are into active defense. "I don't control him. He's free to do what he likes."

"You're obstructing me."

"Because you're acting violently and trying to enter my private residence."

"I told you to get out of my way."

"Ma'am, can you do something about him?" I say to his wife over his head.

"Brett, let's go." She recoils as he turns on her, his face blazing.

"You stay the fuck out of this!"

"Alright, we're done here," Wyn says, adding his bulk to mine. "Ma'am, get your husband out of here before we have to call the cops."

"Brett, you're making things worse," she hisses, finally managing to catch his arm. "We'll call Theo on the way home."

"Hear that?" he says, throwing out his chest. "You kids better get yourself a good lawyer, because this isn't over."

"Drive safe," Karl says, waving as Reagan's dad harries his wife across the street towards the parking enforcement officer who's slipping a yellow ticket under the windshield of their BMW. More drama, as Reagan's dad grabs the ticket and throws it limply at the officer, who grins as he tips his head to speak into his walkie. As much as I'd love to kick back with a beer and watch the cops get involved, Reagan needs me.

If I can find him. All three of us look, plus Gurdeep, who searches the basement that no one ever goes in, and then his own apartment just in case Reagan slipped past us. It's not until I check the bathroom for the third time that I think to look behind the shower curtain, and only because of the smell.

"Just fuck off, okay?" Reagan croaks as I draw back the curtain. He's huddled on his knees, his head hung over the drain, vomit spattering the sides of the tub.

"Shit…" I yank my t-shirt collar up to cover my nose then slap the switch for the fan. I can't handle the smell of puke, no matter what I do. I shout for Karl who comes thundering up the stairs and bursts into the apartment. He smells it at once, his nose wrinkling.

"Grab the paper towels and some clothes," he orders, stripping off his sweater like he's going into surgery.

"I tried so hard," Reagan sobs, clutching the side of the tub. "I couldn't stop it."

"It's okay, sweetie," Karl says as he crouches beside him. "We'll take care of you."

"Your father's gone," I say through my inadequate mask.

Reagan nods but can't answer, and as Karl gets up to wet a washcloth I go and do what I was told, happy to play gofer if it gets me away from the smell. And from making Reagan feel even worse about what was probably a terrible experience.

"Is he okay?" Wyn asks as I come out of the bathroom after dropping off the bundle of clean clothes.

"He was sick to his stomach. Karl's with him."

"I wondered when I heard the shower."

We wander to the living room and each fall into the nearest chair. Our perfect week has turned into a shit-show. And though I want to tell Reagan off for not letting his parents know what happened to him, I can't blame him for keeping them in the dark. If I was him, I'd probably never speak to them again.

TOGETHER

WYN

I'VE NEVER BEEN ARRESTED. Come close a couple times, back when I was younger and mouthier and Toronto cops were still carding hard. Reagan's dad, though... If he'd rushed the door they'd still be picking his teeth up off the sidewalk. It would have been worth it.

"Well, that explains pretty much everything about our boy," I say as I stretch out my legs, tucking my hands behind my head as I settle into their cushy old couch, faking a calm I don't feel as the the adrenaline still hums through my body.

"Imagine growing up with those people?" Carter says, rubbing the bridge of his nose.

"Poor rabbit never had a chance."

"But now what do we do?" He doesn't mean today but tomorrow, and all the days after that.

"I don't know. I didn't think I was ready to care about anyone, not yet. I still think about Pascal all the time. I don't know if I want to let go of that." As Carter bows his head I swallow the lump in my throat. Maybe that's what grieving truly is, carrying this pain with me forever.

Loving him—losing him—will always be a part of me. but I can't let it keep me from living.

"Pascal was a great guy," Carter murmurs. "He didn't deserve to go down like that."

"What are you gonna do? Cancer's a bitch."

The bathroom door scrapes open and we jump to our feet, crowding the doorway as Reagan shuffles out into the hall looking very small and sad, his hair plastered to his skull, his eyes hollow. He gives us a shaky smile, sniffing as new tears gather on his lashes. I'm afraid to touch him, in case he breaks, in case that's not what he wants, until he reaches for me. For us, grabbing Carter's hand too and pulling us into a messed up mash of a hug, Reagan pinned between me and Karl. Laughing through his tears.

"Thank you," he squeaks. "No one's ever taken my side against him."

"He can kick rocks," Karl says, meaning something far less friendly. "No father should treat his son like that. You are a treasure and he is a class-a moron." He plants a kiss on Reagan's cheek.

"Karl, come on," I say with a guilty laugh. "You don't need to be shit-talking him."

"Yes, you do," Reagan says. "Go on, tell me something else you hate about him."

"I'd rather talk about all the things I like about you," Karl says to him with a wicked smile.

"Save it for later. When I'm not starving."

"Weren't you sick just now?" Carter asks him as we untangle.

"From anxiety. And a little bit from sitting in the back of the car, but whatever. So is there anything here to eat?"

In the end we walk down to the Ali Baba's on Queen St. I'm worried that Reagan will overdo it, but he orders a chicken shawarma salad and takes his time eating it. Or is that just from the tension of all of us crowded around this rickety table, watching each other, watching him.

"Okay, you're doing it again," Reagan says, jamming his plastic fork into a chunk of chicken. "Eye-fucking each other. I don't care if you guys are into each other, but you should just come out and say it, right?"

"I don't think that's what's going on," Karl says as Carter falls back in his chair with a groan. "Rather, there's some conversations we all must have that no one has the balls to start."

"We are in a restaurant," I add as Carter nearly chokes. "I don't know that I want to really be talking about this here."

"There'll be plenty of time on the way back to the cottage," Reagan says. "What? Are we not going back?" he asks as we exchange glances. "Come on, we can't let that asshole ruin our vacation. I'll even drive. Unless you all got something better to do."

"Not me," I say with a grin.

"Me neither," Carter said.

"Hell yes," Karl crows. "Our chariot awaits!"

Reagan and I wait by the truck while the others go lock up the apartment. "Be for real with me for a minute," he says, hooking his fingers through my belt-loops to pull me near. "What was going on in the shawarma place?"

"Nothing, but it's like Karl said, we have to talk about a few things before this gets any heavier." I grab his hips to keep him from rubbing against me, but it just makes him squirm more. "Hey there, behave yourself, bunny."

"Or what?" he says, fluttering his lashes.

"Or I'll put you in time out."

"I'll be good!" he yelps, jerking away from me, but I don't let him go far.

"I know you will. Good boys get treats."

"They sure do."

I can't help it, his sassy mouth is right there. I kiss him, trying hard not to grind him against the side of the truck, pulling away when he tries to wrap his leg around my waist. "Chill, bunny. Don't get us in trouble."

I get into the truck and he joins me in the front. The others can have the back. I want this one near me. I want to get him talking, now that he's feeling safer. I want him to feel special, like he matters to me, because he does, in some way that's unlike anything I've felt before. I loved Pascal, but I don't know if I could have shared him. Reagan's different. He was never wholly mine, already partly in love with Carter when he showed up at my place. Somehow I don't care.

"What do think about coming to my place for a few nights when we get back?" I ask him as he flips through the satellite radio channels.

"Yeah, I probably should give these guys a break," he chuckles.

"Not that so much as me wanting a chance to get to know you better."

He settles on some low fi beats and sits back, tucking his hands inside his sleeves. "I want that too," he says with a quiet little smile. "I don't just mean you, I mean that I don't even know myself very well. I spent so many years turning myself into what I thought he wanted me to be. When that all went away, I didn't have a whole lot left."

"You're going to be okay, Reagan. You're a good person."

"Thank you," he whispers as tears well up. "I never thought that would matter so much, but thank you."

I reach across the console to put my arm around his shoulder. He's shaking, but he's breathing, as he uncurls his hands and lays them on his thighs. We sit like this—him breathing, me rubbing his back—until the others join us. We've got so much to talk through, but it can wait until we're at the cottage, sitting around the fire, fed and happy, free of worry. When we can open our hearts to one another, confess our longings and our fears, find a way to make this work so no one feels less than.

We are all more than. Together, we are stronger. We alone are the ones who can define ourselves to ourselves. Shape this growing love into something we all want. Maybe it won't last forever, but nothing ever does. Love, hate, fear, shame, triumph, disaster: all come to an end. Love isn't automatic, it's something you renew every day, with every choice. This choice is ours to make.

"One last stop at my place," I say as we pull away from the curb. "I want to grab a few things. Maybe some quality lube. Just saying, I'm too old to be making do with hand lotion and spit," I add as the others sputter in shock.

It's slow going until we're out of Toronto, but soon the road clears. Midweek we'll miss the worst of the cottage traffic and should be there in time for sunset. I hope riding in the front seat helps Reagan's stomach settle as he naps on and off against the car door. Sucking on his cuffs, his head cradled by Carter's balled up sweater, he's so vulnerable, so desperately in need of someone to take care of him that I'm grateful when Karl demands we pull over for a pit stop, so I can wipe my teary eyes.

I want to take care of him, this restless, damaged kid who fell into our lives. Make my home a place where he feels safe, even if he isn't mine alone. He needs extra love, this casualty of toxic masculinity. At least until he's healed. But as for now, this is enough. This community of mutual care.

Stopping the truck woke Reagan, and he spends the rest of the journey in a growing state of anxiety, chewing at his sleeves, fidgeting with the seatbelt, the door handle, his lip. I want to comfort him but the best thing for all of us is to get our asses back to the cottage as quick as we can. Back to the serenity, and the privacy.

At last we're creeping down the rustling green tunnel of Iain's road. The minute I put it in park, Karl jumps out, groaning as he stretches his legs wide. "Who among us smells the worse, do you think?" he asks as the rest of us get out more slowly.

"All of us, after that sweaty ass car ride," I say, adjusting my junk to unstick it from my thigh.

"There's only one solution for a sweaty ass," Karl crows. He kicks off his shoes then tries to scoop Reagan up in his arms.

"Karl! Your back," Carter shouts, darting forward. Between them they pick up a squealing Reagan and start for the water.

"You better not throw me in, you motherfuckers!"

"Karl, still got my shoes on, bro!"

The trio veers to the right, thundering down the dock and setting Reagan down a few feet from the end. By the time I reach them Karl's naked, and with a cheesy thumbs up he cannonballs into the neck deep water, splashing us all.

"For fuck's sake, Veselko," Carter sputters, wiping his face.

"Oh well, too late now," Reagan says with a sigh as he peels off his clinging t-shirt. Why rock the boat, and in a few minutes we're all in the water, hooting from the chill. I don't care how cold it is, the lake is killing it right now, the sky crystalline, the cliffs and peaks of the Bruce standing out in hi res, the sun cutting a golden path across the lightly ruffled water as we gather in a loose circle on the nearest sandy patch.

"You doing okay?" I ask Reagan as he grips my arm.

"I'm wide awake and my nuts are in my ribcage but yeah, I'm good," he says tensely. "But I need to talk to you. All of you at once. Fuck..." Trembling but not just from the cold, he shuts his eyes, his lips moving as he starts to count under his breath

"Poor zečić," Karl murmurs, wading towards us, but Reagan throws up his hand.

"Don't touch me! I mean, just...just let me get through this one on my own." He closes his eyes again, breathing through his nose, his chest rising and falling, his grip on my arm easing as his panicky tension dissipates.

"Are you good?" I ask him when he opens his eyes.

He nods. "I'm good. And I need all three of you to agree to something."

"Sure thing, Reagan," Carter says. "Tell us what you need."

"Okay. Okay, you have to promise that you're not going to fight about me. That if you start freaking out about something, like you think I'm not giving you enough time, or the other guy's fucking you over, then deal with it, okay? Don't ignore the problem."

"Of course, bunny," Karl says. "We're all adults, yes?"

"You have to promise. All we have between us is our word, Karl. Promise me, or... well you just have to, okay?"

"I understand. I promise, I won't ever hide from you."

"I promise to be honest," I say to Reagan as he turns to me. "To be thoughtful. To trust you. To trust all of you." I meet my friends' eyes in turn, these men I love like brothers. I know what commitment means to them. That's what this is, our promise to each other to do everything we can to make this work for everyone.

It's going to work, because I've never seen Carter smile like that. Like it's coming from somewhere deep inside, without a hint of reservation. I've watched him chase happiness for years, turning sour as it slipped through his grasp. As much as Reagan needs healing, he's healing all of us.

"You're unbelievable," Carter says to him, shaking his head.

"Me? What did I do?"

"Nothing much. Just turned over everything I knew about myself."

Reagan's grip tightens on my arm, his whole body trembling, but I don't think it's from the cold of the water. "I did not."

"I don't like guys like you, remember?" Carter says, wading nearer.

"Duh, I don't even like guys like me."

"Except I don't think that's who you are. Now you're just yourself. The man you always were, behind the fear, the self-loathing."

"There's still a bit of that."

"Healing takes time," he says kindly, sinking in the water until he's facing Reagan eye to eye. "You only separated from your narcissistic father a few hours ago. You'll be ok."

"I know I will. Because I have you guys to help." He breaks then, but it's beautiful, as with a sob he lets me go to leap into Carter's open arms. His joy is my joy, is our joy.

I promise, Reagan," Carter murmurs, "this is for real. This is...this is something I never thought I'd have. This feeling..." It's more than he can put into words as he buries his face in the curve of Reagan's neck. Holding on for dear life.

"Oh my god, you guys, come here," Reagan gasps, beckoning to us. We crash like waves in a crushing group hug, Karl kissing every cheek in reach, Reagan laughing through his tears. This wild young man didn't come between us, he brought us closer together.

Damn, those bronies might be onto something. Friendship really is magic.

RAIN

REAGAN

Six months later...

Losing everything was the best thing to ever happen to me. The money, the toys: they never made me feel half as worthy as these brave men's love. Brave to put their friendship to the test, to put me at the center of their lives.

I sound like a motivational meme but it's true that sometimes you have to lose yourself to find yourself. That's why people say it. You'll never learn who you really are if you keep yourself distracted by all the bright shiny objects capitalism throws at you.

Yes, I'm making this political, but I've learned too much to keep pretending that politics doesn't affect us all, every minute of the day, from banal structural shit like how many crosswalks your city has to massive social statements like who you're allowed to love. Canada's pretty good on both counts.

Which is why I feel safe participating in a gang bang. If by participating I mean letting six or seven men, some of whom I've never met, do whatever they want with my mouth for a hundred and twenty minutes. Mostly I'm just going to kneel there and take it. The fact that it's really happening is hard to believe, minutes before it's meant to start, in the back room of Wyn's little house.

"Are you scared?" Carter asks me, adjusting the straps on the harness I'm beginning to feel really self-conscious about wearing. The whole fit is over the top, consisting of the black chest harness, a black jockstrap, the collar Carter gave me for Christmas, and my newly healed (and only) tattoo: three spiraling teardrops over my heart.

"Does it matter if I'm scared?" I say, my voice cracking.

"Of course it matters," he says, stroking my hot cheek. "Maybe you don't want to be scared."

"I don't really know what I want out of this. Sorry that I can't explain it better."

"It doesn't matter. You're allowed to just want something, bun-bun. You don't have to dust off the Freud to try and explain what makes you want it."

"But isn't it kind of fucked up, to like one thing so much?"

"Bunny, you're not weird," he says, laughing as he cups my chin. "As an elder gay, trust me." He kisses me quickly on the lips then lets me go.

"You're not that old," I say as he checks his watch.

"It's all relative. And if we ever break up—"

"We won't."

"But if we do, promise me you'll protect yourself. I don't want to find out you're sick because you didn't bother to use the health care that prior generations died for not having access to."

"Gee, thanks for getting rid of my boner."

"I'm sure that's not going to be a problem for long."

The front door opens, and a chorus of male voices greets whoever came in. Niobe, the homeowner, who goes about collecting the men's signatures before passing through the sliding door that separates the two halves of the renovated coach-house.

"No offense, guys," she says, flipping through the pages on her clip-board, "but this has gotta be the most fucked up thing I've ever built a spreadsheet for."

"I told you it was fucked up."

"Relax," Carter says to me. "It can't be that fucked up or there wouldn't have been a waiting list."

"That right there," Niobe says, pointing a neon green talon at Carter. The first time I met her, I couldn't stop staring. I'd never met a Black goth before, never mind a cyber goth with butt-length rainbow braids and a hundred thousand Instagram followers who threaten to burn down the world if she doesn't upload an Outfit Of The Day reel. She's the only woman who's ever made me hard just by looking at me, but I know she'd destroy me, and not in the ways I like.

"It's all here," she says, handing the clipboard to Carter. "Lab work, waivers, everything. Your boy's good to go." She winks at me, and for once it has the opposite effect, my hard-on shriveling like she put a witch's curse on it.

"Don't forget that you can stop at any time," Carter says, setting his strong hands on my trembling shoulders. "These people under-stand consent."

"Even if I revoke it while I'm choking on a dick?" I'm making stupid jokes. I'm more nervous than I thought, but he takes it in stride.

"Yes, even then. What's your hand sign?"

I show him my half-fist, the ring and pinky finger extended. One of my guys is meant to be watching for it at all times, to call red light and bring the scene to an end. I'm as safe as I'm going to get. But even if I lose my shit completely, I know the three of them will carry me through the messy parts of healing without shaming me.

"Thanks for all this," I say as Carter fetches my kneepads. "For taking me seriously. Letting me have this. I don't know that anyone's ever done something this nice for me."

"An interesting choice of words," he says, crouching to buckle them on for me.

"Look, growing up, I was given everything, right? Money, education, white cis straight privilege, all of it. So whenever it came to something I personally wanted but that they didn't want me to have, they could just point at everything they'd given me and say, isn't that enough?"

"And it wasn't?"

"You know it wasn't. They were just things. Shoes and toys and cars, watches that cost more than some people's salary. Just ways of showing off. And showing off is just a way of proving you're a loser. Hey, look at all my cool stuff. But when it was something that mattered to me, I didn't deserve it. So I stopped asking. Stopped telling them things about my life. That scene outside the apartment last summer was the first time I'd told them I'm gay."

"Wow."

"Right? I actually thought it was going to go a lot worse. At least I finally got to tell them to go to hell." I don't want to cry right now but talking about my parents still cuts me up. That Christmas card I got from them with a fifty dollar bill in it was one of the biggest insults I've ever received, and I've been to prep school.

"Maybe this isn't the right time for you to do this scene," Carter murmurs, stroking his thumb across my cheeks to wipe away my tears.

"It's exactly right. I've wanted this for so long. Since before I knew it's what I wanted. Please, daddy. Let them fuck me up."

"Goddamn..." He shivers the way he sometimes does when I ask for something extra slutty. Holding my gaze, one hand on my throat above my collar, he feels down the front of me until he reaches my jutting erection. "You're going to keep on surprising me, aren't you?"

"Hope so."

"Let's go, rabbit. Let's see you get what you want."

Music is playing, some wordless pulsing beat. As I close my eyes, Carter rests his forehead against mine. We lean into each other, my arms around his waist, his hands on my shoulders, a calming ritual that invented itself, that helps both of us, because Carter has his own traumas, things he kept quiet about at first, until he knew he was safe.

Safe: I finally know how that feels, though I still have to remind myself, sometimes out loud, that even when I'm scared, whatever's scaring me isn't going to last. I'll be safe again. I trust all three of my men. My circle of lovers, my best friends, my peace.

Here they come to disturb that peace, as the sliding door opens again. I focus on Carter as the men file in, not sure how much I want to remember about the strangers' faces. Toronto's queer and kink scenes are small enough that there's a non-zero chance I'll see them again around town. I was offered a blindfold but I don't like that even with one person. It doesn't matter now, as the lights dim and the music rises and Carter presses down on my shoulders to make me kneel.

Clothes are falling to the floor, bodies moving in my peripheral view, as Carter steps back and unzips his jeans. I moan at the sight of his bulge, the wet patch of precome soaking through his briefs. My mouth is watering, because no matter how many times we do this, I want to do it again. Want to feel his thickness between my lips, filling my mouth, bruising my throat. Want to hear him praise me, offer me his come, however I want to take it. Want to be their darling pet, and I shiver as I feel Karl's hand on the back of my neck, knowing it's him by his smell and by the brush of his hairy leg against my arm. Wyn's inky skin is easy to pick out, though one of the other men is Black too. Niobe's bisexual husband Eric I suspect, from the white-work tattoos across the back of his hand as he squeezes his long, curving dick. So much for anonymity, but if he's not embarrassed, neither am I.

A buffet of dick, all I can eat, every one unique. Spoiled for choice, but I don't need to choose. All I need to do is open my mouth.

They use me, and they use me, and I never want them to stop. Every dick really is unique, each one stretching my lips and jaw in a different way, each man with his own scent, his own taste, his own sounds, his own way of responding to my licking and sucking. Some like to take their time, the way Wyn does, painting my lips with the tip then inching in slowly, teasing me until I want to grab his hips and mount him on my face. Some fuck me fiercely, holding me by the hair, bruising the back of my throat. I love it all, especially the end, because when I was getting ready they agreed to hold off their orgasms, to give me all their come at once.

A symphony of voices, grunting, groaning, moaning, swearing, and the wet slap of their stroking hands; a cascade of come, a rainstorm, each hot and salted drop sizzling as it strikes my skin. My body responds helplessly, my hips jerking as a wave of blazing sensation races through me. Alchemy, like Karl said, that all it takes to get me off is another man's come.

Except there's six of them tonight, their climaxes following one after the other so that there's always a dick in my face, always a new taste striking my panting tongue, always more come. Some of them go around twice, the cheaters, but I'm past caring as I sway on my knees, their come dripping from my chin, my own come leaking down my thighs, my lips swollen, my throat and jaw aching, my mind at peace.

A slut, a pet, an object. Nothing but this body, beyond all time and commerce, absolutely free.

For the first time in my life, it's enough.

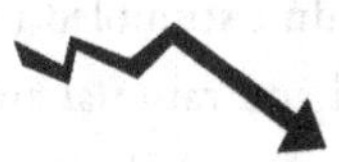

Read on for the holiday short story
A TRICKLE DOWN CHRISTMAS

A TRICKLE DOWN CHRISTMAS

REAGAN

ONCE UPON A TIME, I hated Christmas.

The frantic shopping, the ugly decorations, the hypocrisy of worshiping Jesus *and* Santa and demanding gifts from both of them at the same time. Even the food: ritualized carb loading to bulk you up for the long harsh winter that doesn't even exist anymore. Plastic snowmen on bare lawns, and three days at my parents' place. In other words: Hell.

That was before I made what could have been the worst decision of my life. If I hadn't stumbled into someone as sweet as Carter, as well-informed and rational and kind, if I'd met some other random guy and let him fuck my face behind the bushes at the rec center...I don't want to finish that thought. You all know what can happen to gay guys who choose wrong.

What might have been the worst decision—inasmuch as I made a decision instead of drunkenly grabbing the first man I saw—has turned into the best choice I could have made. That one night changed my life.

Christmas at Carter and Karl's is like what every toy commercial wants you to expect. Not just because Karl has blinged out the living room like a department store display, with branches of greenery hung above every door, a whole-ass village of miniature Victorian houses spread out on the mantelpiece. Every day this week he's worn a different ugly sweater, like the one he has on today of a flight of reindeer towing a sleigh, with little bells stitched to the harnesses so he jingles as he walks.

What really makes this Christmas like nothing I've experienced is his unstoppable joy, as if *Elf* had cast Jack Black instead of Will Ferrell. Maybe not that over the top, but I can hear him singing (and ringing) all the way from the kitchen as I hide in my room, putting the tags on the gifts I bought the guys.

That's something else I've never done, bought someone a present without them telling me exactly what they wanted. None of the three of them asked me, so I went with my best guesses, which is how you're supposed to do it, right? Taking a chance that you guessed wrong, hoping that you've read the other person right, that you're not going to make them laugh or frown or throw your gift away.

And I had to do that for three boyfriends. Sometimes being the center of this messy love feels like work. But nothing good ever comes easy, despite what I used to believe about the economy and my ability to exploit its fringe benefits. Once upon a time, my greatest fear was going broke. Now that that's happened, I've learned there are far worse things to lose than money.

When I hear a knock at the door I leave my room to answer. Wyn greets me with a hug that sweeps me off my feet.

"Merry Christmas to you too," I gurgle, my face squished against the damp shoulder of his coat.

He sets me down then retrieves a small, flat present from his coat pocket and hands it to me. "Merry Christmas, Reagan."

"I'll put it under the tree."

"There's a tree?"

"Dude, there's a little of everything."

He leaves his coat and shoes then brings his bag into the living room where he stops dead. Along with the evergreens and Santa's mini-village, there's a red throw on the couch to go with the green covers Karl put on the throw pillows, garland wrapped around the base of the tv and trailing from the window frames, snowflake decals all over the glass, and a teetering 'pencil' tree that Karl ordered from that chain craft shop and set up in the corner beside the couch.

"I've elbowed decorations off it about a dozen times," I tell Wyn as he cautiously sets out his gifts among the others clustered at the base of the skinny tree, which leans over the couch like Dr. Seuss drew it, occasionally dropping bits of tinsel.

"When Karl loves something, he goes hard."

"I heard my name," Karl calls from the kitchen. "You better be saying nice things about me, or it's lumps of coal for both of you." He appears in the doorway wearing his gingerbread man apron, carrying a tray with four little stemmed glasses, each a different colour.

Wyn groans, clutching his forehead. "Already, man? I just got here and you're trying to get me juiced."

"You'll be fine," Karl scolds. "Eat something to soak it up. Carter, come."

Shaking his head, Carter joins us, drying his hands on the bottom of his plain black apron, which I'm pretty sure he lifted from the bar where he works. He takes the last glass from Karl's tray and we raise them in a toast.

"To new friends and old," Karl says, beaming at each of us. He and Carter toss their drinks back like a shot. Me and Wyn sip ours; Karl's plum brandy tastes like candy and fucks you up like slamming a double vodka and Red Bull (don't ask me how I know.)

"Can I help at all?" I ask as he and Carter return to the kitchen.

"No, no. We've got it under control. You relax."

"They've been saying that for two days," I mutter to Wyn as the others start bickering about the stuffing. "I'm starting to feel kind of useless."

"That's okay, you can keep me company. How are those old weights of mine?" he asks as we settle on the couch.

"Right now they're under my bed because..." I gesture at the Christmas wonderland, including the dining table, laid with a green and gold tablecloth and the closest the house has to matching place settings.

"I forgot they even had a table," Wyn says with a laugh.

"I give it six weeks before it disappears again."

"How's it going, living here?"

I shrug, because it's rude to talk about your friends behind their back. "It's okay. My room is pretty small. Plus the bathroom sucks. If we all had nine-to-five jobs it'd be a warzone, trying to get out the door in the morning."

I don't mention Carter scolding me for not putting away the dishes in the drying rack, or Karl's hair clogging the shower drain, or all the other petty things that must be part of every shared living situation. It might help if my bedroom wasn't basically a closet, just wide enough for a futon and a lamp and a tripod, leaving me nowhere to hang out other than the living room. I've been here for six months and I still feel like a guest.

Our fireplace doesn't work so Karl has the TV on the fireplace channel, the flickering light catching on the gold garland and making Wyn's skin glow as he watches the flames. Out of the three of them,

I'm most at ease with him. Karl is unpredictable: half gentleman, half horn-dog, opening the door for me then grabbing my ass when I pass. Carter is a classic daddy: loving but stern, quick to correct me, careful with praise.

Wyn is just Wyn: warm, kind, funny, focused. Incredibly patient with me when I say something racist, which happens more than I want to admit. Unpacking a lifetime of prejudice doesn't happen overnight. I've accepted that it will take me the rest of my life.

One more reason I'm glad to be here and not at my parents' place. I've heard from my mom twice since I cut them off. I answered her as briefly as I could, just so she knew I wasn't dead. As for my father, I don't expect to ever speak to him again. His loss.

BALDWIN

There's the plans you make, and then there's what the universe wants for you. After losing Pascal to cancer, I was ready to stay single. I'd loved and lost, and I know they say that's better than not doing either, but grieving had taken a lot out of me without putting anything back in.

I had made my peace with an unpartnered future. With being content with myself, maybe hooking up now and then when I needed that itch scratched. When I went out of town, so I wouldn't give the guy the idea that I wanted anything more.

And then Karl dropped this desperate, damaged white boy on my doorstep, with his frosted hair and fucked up family, and now I'm goddamn stuck with him. Stuck because I can't let him go.

Maybe it's because he's not totally dependent on me that it works so well. Caring for Pascal in his last months was terrifying, because of what it did to him and what it did to me: made me doubt my every move, question my every thought, chase answers that didn't exist because I didn't like the ones I'd found. I lost friends, or rather, I found out who in my circles I could count on.

Karl and Carter came through for me time and again, which must have something to do with why our polycule with Reagan works so well. I don't just trust them with myself, I trust them with the man I love.

"What's on your mind?" Reagan asks, snuggling closer on the couch. He's wearing that oversized cashmere sweater he found at the thrift shop last week, and with his knees tucked under it he's a soft grey cloud clinging to my arm.

"Nothing much." I lace our fingers together, his pink and slender, mine brown and callused, thanks to that climbing course I'm taking. "I feel like I haven't seen you in a while."

"I've been slammed. The page is really taking off."

"I gotta say, I never saw you for a Bookstagrammer."

"Me neither. But I guess people like the fact that I've read like five books ever."

"Until now."

He laughs, because I haven't seen him once in the last few months where he hasn't been gushing about the latest book he's read. His social media growth has been surreal, and makes me wish I had half as much engagement, or at least some way to do a collab with him, but there's not a lot of crossover between the functional fitness and gay book content spaces.

Then again, considering what I'm about to ask him, it might not be the worst thing to keep our careers separate. Carter and Karl are yammering in the kitchen, and I'm about to shoot my shot when Karl comes marching out with that damn tray of glasses again, Carter following.

"The bird is resting," Karl announces as he presents the tray to us with a bow. "We have just enough time for presents before we eat."

"Good, because much more of this and I'm going to be lit up like that tree of yours."

As Karl takes the glasses back to the kitchen, Reagan slides off the couch and settles on the carpet by the tree. "I'll pass out the presents."

I don't give gifts to my other friends, but the first year I knew Karl, he lost both his parents, his mom to a car crash and his dad eight weeks later from a heart attack. With no other family in Canada, I made sure he had a good Christmas, and we've kept up the tradition ever since. This year I've signed him up for a scented candle subscription that matches the smell to a famous book. He gives me books, like he gives everyone, sorting me out with an Octavia Butler box set. Carter gives me a nice lightweight tripod I've seen everywhere on photography blogs, and I give him the collected works of Kevin Smith on Blu-ray.

Reagan watches us, handing out the gifts and collecting the used wrapping but not saying much. I hope he's not calculating how much we all spent. This isn't a competition, we're just grown adults with jobs who can drop a couple hundred bucks now and then.

"I hope I did this right," he says as he passes Carter and Karl their gifts. "I've never really bought presents for anyone."

"Not even your parents?" Carter asks.

Reagan rolls his eyes. "My dad just sends me a link. You buy him what he asks for or...well you just do, right? And mom always said she was happy with flowers and some perfume. They never needed anything. Point is, I don't really know what I'm doing."

"I'm sure you did fine, zečić," Karl says as Reagan passes me a sparkly green gift bag. Inside under a ton of crushed red tissue paper is a hard, lumpy object also wrapped in tissue. I peel it open to find the carved wooden figurine of a beaver that I'd admired at a First Nations craft fair Reagan and I visited on our solo trip to the cottage. I'd walked away from the stand thinking I didn't need any more objects filling my home, and especially not when I was getting ready to move, but the carving's little face had stuck in my mind.

"When did you buy this?" I ask.

"Remember I made you stop the car so I could go to the bathroom before we had to drive for an hour? I went back to that booth."

"And you hid it all this time? You sneak. I love it."

"I love you."

I reach for him and he shuffles to me on his knees for a one armed hug. "I love you too, bunny. Now go open the one from me."

"Ugh, you didn't have to get me anything else," he says as he crawls back to the tree.

"Those weights are a hand me down, not your present. And that's not the point of giving gifts. Come on, lemme see you open it."

Blushing, he tears off the wrapping around the small, flat box. Shooting me a dirty look, he pries off the lid. "Holy shit..."

"Do you like it?"

His eyes are shining with tears as he lifts the vintage watch out of its case. "Oh my god, it's so cool."

"It's sure not the one you showed me. The one you gave to that guy at the bus stop."

"The Breitling?" he says vaguely as he lays the Art Deco watch over his wrist. "Fuck that trash, this is for real. Plus it's from you. That makes it priceless."

KARL

So far Christmas is everything I dreamed. The apartment is beautiful, the food will be superb, and Reagan is the happiest I've ever seen him. When he wasn't on his knees drenched in our cum, that is. Oh holy night, and hopefully we all have the good sense not to stuff ourselves silly on turkey, because there's nothing I'd like better than to have him for dessert.

"There's one more thing," Wyn says as Reagan carefully returns the watch to its case. "Something I wanted to ask you."

The room is suddenly silent, save for the soft crackle of the televised flames. Wyn swallows hard, his face heating as we wait for him to speak. Leaned forward on his knees, he clears his throat.

"I've decided to move out of the coach house," he says, speaking to us all but looking at Reagan. "I don't know when because I haven't found a place yet, but I wanted to know if you'd consider sharing with me."

"Me, live with you?" Reagan squeaks, blinking.

I don't want to steal you from these guys, but I thought you all might want a bit more space."

"Oh my god, you want me to live with you?" Biting his lip, he covers his face, his shoulders shaking with emotion.

"I'd be looking for a place on this side of town," Wyn continues. "All my clients are on the west side, and my friends. So we'd still see plenty of each other."

"Oh my god, yes," Reagan gulps from behind his hands. "I mean that's okay with you, isn't it?" Tears shining on his cheeks, he looks from me to Carter and back. Desperate for approval, like he so often is, and I've made it my duty to never deny him.

"I won't pretend that I won't miss you," I say, "but this apartment was never meant for three."

"I'll come see you all the time, I promise."

You won't need to worry. I'll not let you go that easily."

"Carter?"

"I want you to do what's best for you," he says, his voice rough. "This was only ever meant to be temporary, remember?"

"I know. But I really do like living here. I hope it's been okay."

"It has been an honor," I say.

"And who knows how long it'll take me to find a place we can afford," Wyn adds. "You could be here for a while yet."

"Speaking of being here for a while," I say, "let's get these presents opened. Dinner won't be long."

"Then you can go next," Reagan says, bouncing on his knees. "I asked the people at your store, so you can blame them if I fucked up."

"Hmm, nice and thick. Feels good in my hand," I say, hefting the book-shaped gift and making him giggle and Carter groan.

"Just open it, you freak," Wyn says, chuckling.

It is in fact a book, but it still surprises me, because I have never coveted a book so, in all my life, like I have this one special edition, with its sprayed edges and silk bookmark and that embossing on the cover beneath the dust jacket. "How in the world...these sold out in minutes."

"Open it."

With the greatest care so as to protect the spine, I lift the cover and flip to the title page. "My God, it's signed. Oh zečić. The shipping cost—"

"Don't ask," he says with a grimace. "Just don't read it in the bath, okay?"

"I shall cherish it as I cherish you."

He blushes, rolling not just his eyes but his whole head, like he does whenever I lay it on thick. "Oh my god, okay. But there's something else in the bag. Something for later."

"When, later?" I say as I pull out an envelope of what feels like photos. "Five minutes from now? Or in the dark of night."

"More the second than the first," he mumbles, his cheeks turning positively fuscia.

"Zečić, you minx."

"Just put them away, okay?"

"I will after you open your present."

I was tempted to wrap each book individually but I didn't want to steal the spotlight. "Ooh, I've heard about this," he says as he tears open the bigger gift to find the first four volumes of *Heartstopper*. "I didn't know they were books too. They probably came first, right?"

He sets them on the floor then opens my other gift, C.S. Pacat's *Captive Prince* trilogy. "Is this some kind of Princess Bride thing?" he asks as he starts to flip through volume one.

"No. No, it is not."

Running his finger down a page, he startles, blinking hard. "Wow. Okay. How about I put these away for now?"

"Ask me nicely and I'll read them to you. A little bedtime story."

"You'd like that wouldn't you?" he retorts with a cheeky grin. "Alright, Carter. Your turn."

CARTER

Along with a nice pair of blacksmithing gloves, Reagan has given me an envelope like the others. I have some idea of what's in there after interrupting his photo shoot last week, so I set it aside for later. Seeing Reagan open my gift will be more than enough stimulation. Knowing what's coming, the others watch quietly as he tears off the paper and opens the box.

"Oh wow..." Whimpering behind his tightly closed lips, he picks up the leather collar, turning it over reverently. "It's the one I showed you," he says in a little voice.

He raises it to read the inscription on the tag, then drops it in the box with a sob. As he covers his face again, I slip off the couch and shuffle across the floor to him. When I touch his arm he gasps then flings himself at me, burying his head in the hollow of my shoulder.

By now I've stopped being surprised when kindness overwhelms him. It's as if no one has ever done anything nice for him in his life. Having met, or at least witnessed his parents, I could be right. He's always afraid that he's not enough, that he hasn't done enough, given enough. I've stopped trying to talk him out of that feeling. What he needs is to experience so many good things that he forgets to feel bad.

"There's a pair of cuffs, too," I say to him. He shivers in my arms, his hip pressing against my hard-on. "Plus one more thing, if you sit up."

"You guys," he sniffles, wiping his eyes on his shoulder. "Seriously, this is too much."

"Hush," says Karl, passing him the envelope. The collar isn't the only way I want to show him that he's ours. If he was a kid, we'd be accused of spoiling him. He deserves it, for having grown so much as a person since we met. For letting go of so many of the beliefs that had fucked up his life in the first place.

Still in my lap, he opens the envelope and pulls out the tattoo shop gift certificate. "Shut the fuck up. You did not. You guys are ridiculous."

"It's not enough to do a sleeve or anything," I tell him. "But it'll cover that design you drew."

"The teardrops? For real? And you're all cool with that?"

Three coloured teardrops spiraling around each other, representing me, Karl, and Wyn. He's been drawing it on everything, whenever he's sitting still and there's a pencil nearby.

"I would be honored," Karl says with his usual sincerity.

"Me too," Wyn says, grinning.

"There's no rush, though," I say. "Whenever you're ready."

"Speaking of ready," Karl says as a timer in the kitchen dings. He hops off the couch and goes to check on whatever it is. I've been playing sous chef, peeling and chopping and stirring and doing whatever else he tells me, but hopefully he won't need me for a few minutes.

"Do you mind trying that stuff on to be sure it fits?" I ask Reagan.

"Mind? Try and stop me, daddy," he says. He wriggles off my lap and grabs the box and follows me to my bedroom. Thanks to him,

I've started keeping it cleaner than I used to, and I only have to move a couple things out of the way of the tall mirror on my dresser.

The new leather is stiff as I help him buckle the cuffs. "They'll soften up once you wear them a little," I say as he runs a finger around the inside of one. "The collar too."

He doesn't reply, his expression blank as I wrap the collar around his throat. He whimpers as I jerk on the buckle. "Too tight?" I ask.

"It's okay for now," he replies, his eyes glassy as he gazes at himself in the mirror. He's breathing too quickly, his chest rising and falling beneath the fuzzy sweater, his face pink and sweaty.

"Do you want to take it off?"

"Can I?" he asks, touching it tentatively.

"Of course."

"I don't want you to think I don't appreciate it," he says as I wrestle with the stiff strap.

"It's okay, bunny. They said it might take some getting used to."

He breathes easier once it's off, touching the red mark it left on his neck. There's tricks to soften leather and I make a mental note to look them up later. There's something else I need to give him first.

"I have one more thing for you," I say, moving closer and putting my hands on his fuzzy hips.

"Oh my god, stop," he groans, turning to put his arms around my neck. "You bought me too much already."

"This isn't that kind of present. I was thinking about that video we were watching the other night."

"Go on..."

"About how hot it made you. And it got me thinking, what if that was you?"

He studies my face, his hips twitching between my hands. "What are you saying?"

"I'm saying, what if I could make that happen for you? Not just the three of us but a whole train of guys jacking off onto your pretty face?"

He shivers, pressing closer, his hard-on nudging mine. "How?" he breathes.

"Niobe and Eric have hosted plenty of events. I'm sure they'll have advice. Plus the three of us would be there so you wouldn't be in any danger."

"Maybe from drowning. But what a way to go."

"That's my little cumslut," I purr as he wriggles against me.

"Damn it, daddy, you got me all horny."

"What are you talking about? You're always horny."

"Guilty as charged."

We kiss because he's so good to kiss. Because he's mine to kiss. To fuck. To share, because I love watching him take a dick deep into his sweet throat. Anyone's dick, not just mine. The fact that I can share him with my two best friends is a miracle. Like this was always meant to be. I was always meant to meet Reagan by accident, to make that one bad decision but have it turn into the best thing that's ever happened. I lift my mouth from his to try and make this swirl of thoughts into something sentimental, but he beats me to the punch.

"Okay, let me try on the collar again," he says, panting hard, his fingers digging into my shoulders.

"Are you sure?"

"No, but let's try anyway."

REAGAN

I cannot believe how badly I want this collar around my neck. Even knowing that it freaked me out just a few minutes ago. That was the past, before I got a grip on my racing thoughts and panicked breathing. Before my body got used to the idea.

Because I trust this man. All three of them. Like I've never trusted anyone before. How could I have trusted when allI knew was my parents' performative morality, and my dad's bitterdisappointment at everything I did. No matter how hard I tried, it was neverenough.

That's in the past too. I'll text my mom on Christmas Day, but I'll never talk to that homophobic piece of shit again. Bitter words when I should be thinking about Carter and the collar and the weight of it settling against my throat. The inside is still raw, the edges scraping my skin, but the look of it is unbeatable, because it proves that I belong to him.

I always knew it was symbolic. No one can own another person. Slavery isn't wrong because it's a crime, it's a crime because it's wrong. And yet we play this game, where I'm his possession. Their possession, that they pass between them. Their pet, who does what he's told. But I do it because I want to, because I want these men to possess me. Use me. Fuck me hard then do it all again.

"Do you want to show the others how pretty you are?" Carter says, lifting my chin so I'll look him in the eye.

"Yes, daddy."

He bites his lip, groaning deep in his throat. "It's going to be hard to keep from taking advantage of you."

"I thought that was the point."

He laughs then plants a kiss on my forehead. "If we skip dinner, Karl will lose his shit." Letting me go, he's about to open the door when he pauses and looks me over again. "One more thing," he says. I'm about to complain again when he grabs the front hem of my sweater and tucks it into the waist of my shorts, showing off my dick which is about five seconds away from shoving its way out of the liner and falling out of one of the legs.

"Perfect."

My feet barely seem to touch the ground as he steers me out of his room and along the hall, my every breath making the collar tighten briefly around my throat. He stops in the doorway to the living room where Wyn is showing Karl his little figurine.

"Damn..." Wyn breathes as Karl swears softly in Croatian. "Merry Christmas to us."

Licking his lips, he rises from the couch, his dick growing before my eyes. "Bunny, you are something else."

"Is it okay?" I ask as he approaches, my voice coming out soft and panting and even more desperate than I feel. But I need to know that this is what he wants too. I want him to want me.

"It's better than okay," Wyn says, smiling as he cups my face. Holding my gaze, he slips his hand down to the thick band of leather. I shiver as he slips one finger between the collar and my throat. Again as he tugs on the collar, pulling me against him.

As he bends to kiss me Carter chuckles. Somehow watching me get railed gives him almost as much pleasure as doing it himself. Yep, there goes his zipper as he opens his fly.

"Well, I suppose the bird can rest a little longer," Karl says. He gets up from the couch with a scraping of springs then joins us.

"Can you take that fucking thing off now," Carter says tiredly.

"Of course," Karl replies. Bells jingle as he pulls off his ugly as fuck sweater. "I'd rather not get everyone else's spunk on it anyway."

Wyn laughs into my mouth. Karl's a goof but I love him so much. I love them all, each in their own way. I don't deserve this much love, but I'm doing my best to believe that I do, that I deserve love as much as anyone else. I know they love me, and they must love each other to be able to share me this way.

A year ago, I thought sharing was for suckers. That compassion was another word for weakness, and love the lie we use to justify desire. I never thought I could be so happy to be wrong. Compassion is a strength: to love someone who is nothing like you, who didn't do a thing to deserve it, who's so wounded he can't help but hurt others. To still love someone who's broken: there is no finer gift.

I was broken, and they still loved me. I was wrong about myself, about the world, and they helped me figure out what's right. Everything I now am, I learned how to be because these men love me.

"Sorry," I say, sniffing away my tears. Even this: that I can cry and they don't deride me, don't tell me to man up, to stop being a child. "I'm just so happy. This is the best Christmas I've ever had. The best year, period. Even if started out rough. You changed my life. All of you. So thank you. For accepting me, for loving me."

I can't go on, sobbing for real, because these feelings are too big to be contained. They understand, murmuring sweet words of encouragement and love, Wyn and Carter both rubbing my back, one high, one low, Karl holding my hands.

"How could we not love you, zečić?" he says softly.

"I don't exactly make it easy," I gulp.

"Paugh. That which comes easily is easily lost. I like that you challenge me. And I'll miss you."

"Me too," Carter says gruffly.

"Aw, stop. I don't want to cry anymore. Also, I'm starving, are we having dinner or what?"

They laugh—we all laugh. Then Carter zips up his fly and Karl orders us into the kitchen, each to carry a dish to the dining table.

It's a tight fit with the four of us and all the food, but I wouldn't have it any other way. This is my family now, these three men who let me into their lives. Who gave me a chance when I had none. Who taught me what life is truly worth, and that love is a gift that never stops giving, that grows and grows the more of it you give away.

I used to want to win. Now I want to care. I used to value money. Now I don't have enough of it for it to matter. What good was all that money when what I really needed wasn't something you can buy?

This is what I needed: this family of friends. This lucky break, this once in a lifetime love. One chance that could have gone so wrong.

It's paid me back with three times the love, and all it cost me was everything. I'd say I got a pretty sweet deal.

MERRY CHRISTMAS!

ACKNOWLEDGEMENTS

Massive shout out to the twisted, thirsty, wonderful bookish community on Threads, whose unchecked craving for this story made it worth writing.

Specific thanks to my amazing beta readers who helped me turn what started as a silly idea into a real book: Amanda Winter, Brianne Law, Becca Mathis, A.R. Millner, and T.L. Hightower.

Personal and eternal thanks to my family who endure my choice of career with grace and enthusiasm even if I can't let any of them read my books.

And thanks to you, because you read this far. Never change.

xoxo

W

ABOUT THE AUTHOR

Author, blogger, and general nuisance Will Forrest writes unusual – and usually queer – Historical and Paranormal Romances with a dash of mischief and mayhem.

Will grew up on a steady diet of Douglas Adams and classic 90s bodice rippers, and has a diploma of fashion design, a degree in social theory, and a bad habit of changing careers, life goals, and continents. Currently they live in a very warm part of Canada with three lovely humans and a succession of martyred houseplants.

willforrest.com

Join the Readers Club for advance access, free books, and (occasionally) recipes.

willforrest.com/newsletter/

WILL FORREST'S BOOKS

HOLLOWOOD FALLS - Disaster gay werewolves in love

LONDON HUSTLE – Bawdy house adventures in the Victorian Demimonde

HOW TO LOVE A LORD – classic Historical Romances with a modern twist

TALES OF ELSEWHEN - a Gaslamp Fantasy Universe where Monsters, Myths & Magic collide

THE LIBERTINES - high-heat Polyam Romance from the Gilded Age

3 DARING DUKES - a series of twisted Regency Fairy Tales

FREE READS - samples and short stories

TRICKLE DOWN THEORY – Contemporary MM+ Why-Choose

AUTHOR, AUTHOR – a Midcentury Gay Romance

COMING SOON

STUCK IN THE MIDDLE – Contemporary MM+ Why-Choose

STARMAN – a '70s High School Love Story

AFTER THE AFFAIR – a collection of Gay Historical Romance novellas

Join the Readers Club for updates & free books: willforrest.com/newsletter/